THE
GHOST WHO
PINCHED ME

Dr. C, Don't Get Pinched !

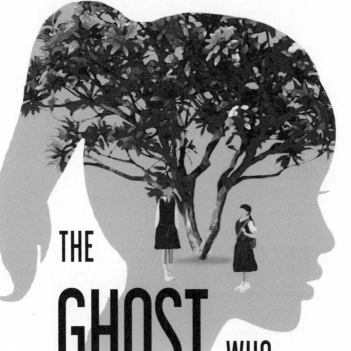

THE

GHOST WHO

PINCHED ME

mabel gan *falllabel*

Marshall Cavendish
Editions

With the support of

NATIONAL ARTS COUNCIL
SINGAPORE

© 2019 Marshall Cavendish International (Asia) Private Limited
Text © Mabel Gan

Published by Marshall Cavendish Editions
An imprint of Marshall Cavendish International

A member of the
Times Publishing Group

Other Marshall Cavendish Offices:
Marshall Cavendish Corporation, 99 White Plains Road, Tarrytown NY 10591-9001, USA • Marshall Cavendish International (Thailand) Co Ltd, 253 Asoke, 12th Flr, Sukhumvit 21 Road, Klongtoey Nua, Wattana, Bangkok 10110, Thailand • Marshall Cavendish (Malaysia) Sdn Bhd, Times Subang, Lot 46, Subang Hi-Tech Industrial Park, Batu Tiga, 40000 Shah Alam, Selangor Darul Ehsan, Malaysia.

Marshall Cavendish is a registered trademark of Times Publishing Limited

National Library Board, Singapore Cataloguing-in-Publication Data

Name(s): Gan, Mabel.
Title: The ghost who pinched me / Mabel Gan.
Description: Singapore : Marshall Cavendish Editions, [2019]
Identifier(s): OCN 1112785017 | ISBN 978-981-48-4188-7 (paperback)
Subject(s): LCSH: Sisters--Juvenile fiction. | World War, 1939-1945--Singapore--Juvenile fiction. | Singapore--History--Japanese occupation, 1942-1945--Juvenile fiction.
Classification: DDC S823--dc23

Printed in Singapore

To my grandmother,
who lost four children
in a Japanese air raid on Singapore

ONE

I remember the first time I saw Ying. She was standing in the back garden, under the frangipani tree. She was wearing her St Mary's school uniform. Her eyes were big and bright. Her hair was straight and shiny, just like always.

It was a terrible day from the beginning. The sky was covered with grey clouds all morning. I did not touch my lunch, which was only a bowl of porridge and a fried egg with salty chye por. Sitting at the big marble table alone, with the simple food that the amahs, our servants, usually ate, I felt sorry for myself. Before I could sneak off, Yong Cheh, our oldest amah, who was fat and had a big, booming voice, pounced on me.

"Cannot eat? Then go upstairs and sleep!" she barked.

"Naps are for children! I'm ten years old," I protested indignantly.

"You have a fever! Your Ma asked me to look after you!"

She grabbed my arm roughly and started pulling me away, so I purposely knocked the basket of buah langsat off the table. The small round fruits bounced and rolled everywhere.

"Aiyah! Si geena," Yong Cheh scolded, as she ran around picking them up one by one.

"Ma says you cannot call me that!" I yelled at her from a safe distance.

"Who said you can raise your voice at me, si geena? Your grandmother will rise from her grave and slap you."

"She will slap you first if she hears you calling me that."

"Aiyoh how dare you! I raised your father from the day he was born."

I'd heard her say this a thousand times already, so I got bored and ran off. I knew that I could get away with anything that day.

I went to Ma's sewing room and opened her cupboard of pretty fabrics. There were bolts of shiny silk from China, transparent Swiss voile in bright colours, and my favourite – delicate Italian lace with beautiful, intricate patterns. Ma had a lot of nice things because Papa was a merchant who shipped all sorts of goods from different countries to Singapore. We always had fancy things at home, like caramel sweets wrapped in gold foil, English biscuits filled with lemon cream, and boxes of chocolates with mysterious centres. I was deciding whether to unroll some fabric to play with, which Ma would surely scold me for doing, when I heard a soft knock at the door. It was Siew Cheh, with a cup of barley water. I loved the sweet drink that she always made for me with a bit of lemon.

Siew Cheh was the youngest of our three amahs and my favourite. Even though we already had two amahs, Papa had taken pity on her and brought her into our home. Ma said that she was an orphan, and bad people had wanted to sell her as a mui tsai or slave girl. Luckily, Mrs Collins, the wife of one of Papa's business associates, had come to her rescue. I loved

Siew Cheh's heart-shaped face with eyes that always seemed to be smiling. Sometimes, when Ma was mean to me, I secretly wished that Siew Cheh was my mother.

Siew Cheh squatted next to me as I drank my barley water. "Bee ah, now that you are ten years old, I think you understand that serious things are happening. Singapore is under attack, and war can come any time."

I nodded quietly.

"Your poor Ma and Papa are going through a hard time. Even though this terrible thing has happened, they still have to worry about you and the baby. And your Ma is not feeling well these days."

I felt hot tears stinging my eyes, so I drank slowly to hide them.

"Bee, you're a clever girl, and you can help your parents. What you should do now is rest and get well quickly." She put the back of her hand gently on my forehead. It felt cool and soothing. "Your fever is still high. Take a nap so you can get well, hor?"

I agreed to take a nap because what Siew Cheh said made sense. That was why I listened to her. Ma and Papa said that I had to respect the amahs because they were my elders. But the other amahs were stupid. Yong Cheh liked to scold and threaten me, and Eng Cheh, who always looked sleepy because of her long, droopy eyes, would try to bribe me or plead with me. I never listened to them because they never gave me any good reason to.

Upstairs in my room, I lay in bed for a long time, but I couldn't fall asleep. Then I heard some strange noises. I looked out of my bedroom window, but the street was empty and quiet. I hurried to the bathroom on the other side of the house.

The window was too high, so I carefully climbed onto the edge of the earthen pot that held the water for our baths.

I couldn't believe my eyes! The three amahs, in their distinctive samfu of white shirt and black pants, were gathered around the mango tree in the back garden. Siew Cheh and Eng Cheh were digging with the gardener's cangkul while Yong Cheh supervised them. I immediately knew what they were doing! They were stealing Ma's jewellery that Papa had buried there just a week ago. He'd said it was to keep it safe in case the Japanese invaded Singapore. I wanted to scream, but I knew that Ma and Papa were not there to hear me, so I watched helplessly, my heart pounding fiercely in my chest.

Sure enough, I saw the amahs lifting the red silk bags out of the ground and dusting them off. Siew Cheh opened one and took out something shiny. She admired it, then held it up to one ear. They all laughed. It made me so angry that tears sprang to my eyes.

Something made me turn from the amahs to the frangipani tree in the corner. And there she was – Ying. She was looking straight up at me. I shivered. Was my fever making me imagine things? I needed to tell Ma and Papa right away, but at this very moment in time, they were at Bukit Brown, tending to Ying's funeral.

TWO

My sister, Ying Ying, was two years older than me. Everyone loved her, especially Ma, but I must confess that when she was alive, I couldn't stand her. Ma said I was jealous, but I thought that Ying was really not that pretty. Anyway, it didn't bother me as much as everyone saying she was so nice. Of course, they didn't know that she liked to pinch me so hard that my skin would turn blue-black. Whenever I complained to Ma, she said that it was my fault for "disturbing" Ying. Ma always took Ying's side. Sometimes, I wondered if I was adopted.

I also thought that Ying was selfish. She didn't like to share her things, and she would make a big fuss if I borrowed anything. One time, I brought her coloured pencils to school because I couldn't find mine. She got angry and complained to Ma. I had only lost the white one, which no one even uses, and the yellow one kept breaking, so I had no choice but to keep sharpening it – it wasn't my fault that it became so short! But, of course, Ma punished me. I had to help Eng Cheh wash the dishes, so I took my revenge and spat into Ying's water bottle – just a little bit, so that no one would notice.

I used to wish that I did not have to go to the same school as Ying. On my first day of Primary One, all the teachers said,

"Oh! Ying Ying's little sister!" And from that day, I became known as Ying's little sister.

Ying was the most popular girl in St. Mary's Primary School. She always topped her level in exams, and on Sports Days, she won a lot of trophies because of her long legs. At school concerts, she played the piano on stage, looking glamorous in the dresses that Ma specially tailor-made for her. That was why everyone in school thought that Ying was really special.

My classmates were always asking me about her. *What is Ying like at home? What does she like to do? What does she wear when she's not in school uniform?* They just couldn't stop talking about her. *She's so pretty! She's so smart! You're so lucky to be her sister!* Well, of course, I couldn't have told them the truth. They would not have believed me if I had said that Ying was an annoying sister. She always acted so nice to me in school. She said hello to me and my friends, and she bought me haw flakes and salted plums from the tuck shop. In turn, I acted like I was the lucky little sister and made my classmates jealous.

This went on until I was in Primary Four, and Ying was in Primary Six. As everyone expected, she became Head Girl. She stopped wearing the ordinary St Mary's uniform with the blue pinafore. Instead, Ying sported a navy-blue skirt and matching vest with a long-sleeved white shirt and red prefect's tie. She was also given a shiny gold pin with the school crest to put on her tie. She was very proud of herself, and I couldn't wait for her to go to secondary school the following year.

A few days before Ying died, we had a fight. I wanted to borrow her prefect's tie for a class play, but she refused to lend it to me.

"Why don't you use one of Papa's?" she asked.

"Because I'm playing a prefect, and he doesn't have a red tie.

Why can't you just lend it to me?"

"Because I only have one, and it's important."

"Everything is important because you're selfish!" I yelled.

She put on her silly, mature voice, "I'm sorry you feel that way, Bee Ling, but I don't trust you because you have a habit of spoiling my things. Or losing them."

"Well, I'm sorry you feel that way, Ying Ying," I imitated her, "but I don't like you because you're selfish and – and stupid!" I stormed out, slamming the door even though I knew that Ma would scold me for waking the baby up.

The next day, I refused to talk to Ying. After school, she came to my room with a packet of salted plums, but I refused to take them.

"I asked Sister Dawn if there's an extra prefect's tie you could borrow for the play, and she said that she would check," Ying said. I continued doing my homework as if she wasn't there. She sighed dramatically and left.

That night, when we were asleep, the air-raid sirens sounded. This had been happening since last Christmas because Japan was attacking Singapore. We were not scared because we knew that the British Army would protect us.

As usual, Ying came to get me. "Bee, wake up!" she whispered.

I held Ying's hand tightly as we walked through the darkness to the bomb shelter that Papa had constructed in the garage. We went in through a small door that was cut into the back wall of the kitchen. It was cramped in there with the eight of us among the sandbags lining the walls – Papa, Ma, Ying, me, the baby and the three amahs. The room was hot and stuffy. We sat on the straw mats covering the floor.

The amahs looked funny in the candlelight. Instead of

their neatly combed hair buns, their hair was loose on their shoulders. Also, they were wearing flowery pyjamas instead of their samfu. I thought that Siew Cheh looked even prettier with her hair down.

Soon we heard the roar of airplanes, and the shrill whistling and thunderous booms of the air raid. My heart thumped in my chest, and I gripped Ying's hand tightly. Eng Cheh was so frightened that she made funny, high-pitched noises. Yong Cheh called her some rude names, but she continued whimpering. The strange thing was that the baby, Ming Ming, who was usually woken up by every little sound, slept through all the noise.

The next morning, we were exhausted, but Papa wanted us to go to school. He said that we should not let the Japanese bullies disrupt our lives. I took a long time to get ready because I was falling asleep on my feet. Ying kept hurrying me. She said that as Head Girl, she could not be late for Assembly.

Papa dropped us off at the school gate just before the final bell. We dashed across the courtyard, but before we could reach the school hall, the bell rang. Ying pinched me so hard that tears came to my eyes. I rubbed my arm where it was already turning blue-black.

Shortly after recess, the air-raid sirens sounded. This had been happening since school started this year, so we already knew what to do. Class by class, we briskly filed into the corridors and made our way to the school hall. Inside the crowded hall, I passed Ying. "Not again," she said, and rolled her eyes playfully. I was still angry with her for pinching me, so I ignored her.

I never saw her again.

Later, our principal, Sister Margaret, explained to Ma and Papa that after the sirens had stopped, Ying led a group of students who wanted to use the toilet out of the hall. That was Ying in school – always a leader. No one suspected that a bomb had fallen on the roof of the bathroom hut across the courtyard, where it sat waiting until the girls entered, and then exploded.

THREE

On the day of Ying's funeral, I kept watch at the window for Papa's car until my legs cramped up. Finally, I saw Papa's white Austin and ran downstairs.

"Papa, you were gone for so long! I have important things to tell you," I said as his car door opened. Papa's handsome face was drawn with worry.

"Bee, I'm afraid Ma is not feeling well."

I followed Papa to the other side of the car. Ma was reclining in the passenger seat with her eyes closed. She looked smaller and paler than usual in a shapeless, black dress. Papa carefully picked her up. He was six feet tall, with broad shoulders and strong arms, so he had no trouble carrying Ma, who was slim and barely five feet.

I knew that this was not the right time to talk to Papa, so I quietly followed him into the house. The amahs were worried when they saw Ma in this state. Quietly, we all filed up the stairs to Ma and Papa's room. Papa gently laid Ma on the bed and instructed Yong Cheh to take care of her. Then he went downstairs to telephone Dr Oei. The amahs left the room, leaving me alone with Ma.

I stared at Ma, not sure if she was asleep. Her eyes fluttered open, and I saw that they were red and swollen.

"Bee, are you still having a fever?" she asked.

"No, it's gone," I lied. "What happened to you, Ma?"

"Oh, just tired. Don't worry about me," Ma said, and closed her eyes.

Yong Cheh returned with a bottle of oil with a black cat on the label. "Don't disturb your Ma," she warned.

"Who says I'm disturbing her?" I answered.

Yong Cheh ignored me and started rubbing Ma's legs with the oil. It smelled horrible, so I left the room.

I wanted to tell Papa about the jewellery and especially about Ying, but he was in the bathroom. The amahs were bustling around as usual. The baby had woken up, and Siew Cheh was feeding him. Eng Cheh usually did the cleaning, but she was cooking dinner because Yong Cheh was busy with Ma. I couldn't believe that they would behave so normally when they had just robbed our family! I wanted to shout that they were thieves, but I decided to wait and tell Papa when I had the chance.

At dinner, I had to eat by myself again. This time, it was rice with a small, fried fish. I refused to eat the fish because it was dry, so I used my chopsticks to poke out its eyeballs. Siew Cheh brought me some pork floss, but I knew that she was only pretending to care. I ignored her and went to look for Papa.

Papa was in his study, and the door was closed. I was about to open it when I heard a strange sound. It was soft at first, but then it got louder. To my horror, I realised that Papa was crying. I never imagined that my brave, strong Papa would cry, and now his loud sobs tore at my heart. I ran upstairs to my room, climbed into bed, and buried my head under the pillow.

For a week now, I had watched Ma and the amahs weeping

over Ying, with the feeling that it was all a dream. Every time I looked up or turned my head, I expected to see her walk through the door. Sometimes, I thought I heard her voice in another room, and then I would remember – Ying was dead. Still, it would not sink in. Ying was the bossy big sister who was always telling me what to do. How could she be gone? Now after hearing Papa's sobs, I finally felt the loss, not only of Ying but of the way that things had been in our home. We had always eaten dinner together – Papa, Ma, Ying and me.

My door softly creaked open.

"Go away," I mumbled, but I heard Siew Cheh come in. She stopped next to my bed, and I felt her hand on my shoulder.

"Go away! I know what you did," I said from under the pillow, but she did not remove her hand. It was a gentle touch and felt cool through my cotton blouse. Slowly, my anger and sadness melted away.

Then I couldn't feel her hand anymore. I lifted my head and was surprised to see that the room was empty. How did Siew Cheh disappear into thin air? And then I knew. It was Ying.

FOUR

The days that followed dragged on from one to the other. I was cooped up in the house with nothing to do. Ma had not left her room since Ying's funeral. Papa was gone for long hours, and when he came home, he would go into his study to listen to the radio about the war. The amahs were strangely quiet. It seemed as if they were walking around on tiptoes and whispering to each other. Perhaps they were planning to steal more things. I decided to keep an eye on them.

I missed going to school. The new school year had only just begun. I was not a top student like Ying, but I enjoyed my classes. My favourite subjects were English and Science. I loved my English teacher, Sister Nira. Her lessons were always so much fun, with games and quizzes, and she let us put on plays. I wondered what she was doing now that school was closed.

I loved Science because we got to visit the school garden to look at the plants and animals. There were eight rabbits and five chickens. I remember the day we found an egg. My best friend, Janet Lim, was the one who had spotted it in the grass. We used some rags to make a little nest for the egg, and Sister Dawn put it under a lamp in the science lab. During Chapel that week, we prayed that a fluffy, yellow chick would hatch from the egg.

Alas, the days went by and nothing happened.

Before long, we forgot about the egg because a four-foot-long monitor lizard came into the school garden and killed two of our chickens, Rusty and Fluffy. The teachers moved all the animals into the science lab, while the school gardener led an operation to trap the reptile. A week later, Sister Margaret announced at Morning Assembly that the monitor lizard had been captured and released into the jungle. The rabbits and chickens were returned to the garden after that.

I wondered what happened to the animals. Did they survive the bombing? My mind kept going back to that last day of school.

We were sitting on the floor in the school hall, singing hymns to drown out the screeching of artillery shells. When the air raid ended, Sister Margaret praised us for behaving well and said we could return to class. As usual, the Primary Six girls left the hall first. We were standing in line, waiting for our turn, when a powerful explosion rocked the ground and flung us on top of one another. I struggled to get myself off my partner, Susie, but others were pinning me down. I could not move, breathe or hear anything.

There was dust in the air, and bits and pieces of white plaster rained down on us from the ceiling. In the midst of this chaos, Pauline from Class 4C caught my eye. Her head was covered in white dust as if she had fallen into a barrel of flour! She looked so funny, but I was too dazed to laugh. Slowly, my hearing returned, and I could make out screaming and crying. At the time, I didn't understand why everyone was so upset.

They kept us in the school hall for a long time. Later, I heard that it was because of the gory scene outside. The Primary Six girls said there was skin and blood all over the courtyard.

Someone even said that there was an arm hanging from the pom pom tree. Nine girls and two teachers died that day.

I overheard Yong Cheh telling the amahs next door that Ying's body was the only one that was returned to the family. The reason they could identify her was because of her red prefect's tie.

St. Mary's Primary School was permanently closed after the bombing.

FIVE

I was tired of being stuck at home, so I insisted on following Siew Cheh on her errands. On a trip to the provision shop, I was waiting for Siew Cheh by the fruit stand outside when I felt a tap on my shoulder. I turned and was surprised to see Katie Harrison. She had been one of Ying's best friends in school.

"Hello, Katie," I said shyly.

She was wearing a simple white dress. Her long blond hair, which she always wore in a ponytail at school, draped over her shoulders. I thought she looked very pretty and grown up.

"How are you, Bee Ling?" Katie asked.

"I'm fine, thank you. And you?" I answered awkwardly.

To my surprise, Katie's eyes welled up. "I miss Ying so much! I still can't believe she's gone," she cried.

I watched helplessly as large teardrops fell from her round blue eyes and rolled down her cheeks. I felt sorry for Katie, and that's why I decided to tell her.

"Can I tell you a secret?" I asked. "It's about Ying."

"Of course," she said, leaning towards me.

"She's still around," I whispered.

"What do you mean?" Katie asked, confused.

"I've seen her in my house, well, in the garden, actually. She's still wearing her school uniform."

Katie stared at me with her mouth open, different emotions passing over her face. Finally, she looked cross. "Bee Ling, I don't know why you're – Is this a joke?"

I felt as if she had slapped me. I wanted to run off, but I was rooted to the spot, my face burning with shame. Katie tossed her beautiful hair and started to walk away.

Out of the corner of my eye, I noticed a tiny movement. A single rambutan dropped from the pile on the fruit stand, bounced twice on the ground, and rolled to a stop at Katie's feet. We both stared at the red, hairy fruit sitting in front of Katie's white shoes. Just as she carefully stepped over it, a dark purple mangosteen fell from the display and rolled into her path. Katie bent down and picked up both fruits. Her eyes were wide as she turned to me.

"Ying's favourite fruit was rambutan. Mine is mangosteen."

"Oh," I replied, not sure what to say.

"We even made up made up a rhyme about it in Primary Two. It goes,

Rambutan, rambutan, mangosteen
Best friends just like Katie and Ying!"

I couldn't help giggling because it sounded so childish. I never imagined that Ying would ever say anything so silly. Just then, Katie's amah came out of the shop carrying several overstuffed grocery bags.

"Ah! Ying Ying's little sister," she said, smiling.

Katie carefully put the rambutan and mangosteen back on the fruit stand. Before she left, she looked me in the eye and said, "Please say hello to her for me."

That night in bed, I thought about my conversation with Katie. I'm glad that she eventually believed me, but I decided not to tell anyone else about Ying. It suddenly occurred to me that Ying was following me around. Snuggling deeper under my blanket, I whispered, "Ying! Ying, can you hear me? Katie says hello."

My heart thumped as I waited for an answer, but I only heard the trees rustling outside my window.

SIX

Papa was buying sacks of rice and storing them in the bomb shelter. He sent the amahs to buy bags of salt, sugar, and flour as well as tins of milk powder. Yong Cheh went to the Chinese medical hall, and two shop assistants had to help her bring home the packages of herbs wrapped in bright pink paper.

When I went to the kitchen for a snack, I was overwhelmed by the sharp smell of salted fish. I also noticed a lot of flies buzzing around. I complained to Papa, and he gave Yong Cheh a wooden box to store the salted fish.

Papa said that food prices had skyrocketed because everyone was stocking up for the war. He said that we should prepare for Singapore falling to the Japanese. British citizens were already leaving Singapore. If Ma was well, we would also try to leave, but she was too weak to travel. He told the amahs not to worry, he would take care of them. Yong Cheh started wailing and saying that she had cared for him from the day he was born and he was like a son to her. I wanted to say right then that I had seen her stealing Ma's jewellery, but I was afraid that without the amahs, there would be no one to take care of us.

Ma was still sick. She hardly left her bed anymore. She was also crying all the time. Dr Oei said that she needed iron pills, but they did not seem to help. The only times she looked better were after Yong Cheh's massages. Yong Cheh also brewed smelly herbal soups for her. If Yong Cheh left, there would be no one to take care of Ma.

Ma had no more milk for the baby, so he had to drink milk made from powder. I helped by feeding him from a baby bottle. I loved the way his mouth clamped onto the rubber teat and made little sucking noises. I thought I was doing a good job because Ming's cheeks were plump and rosy, and he looked like he had three chins. Siew Cheh prepared Ming's milk with hot water, and she boiled the milk bottles and rubber teats on the stove to sterilise them. She also bathed him and changed his diapers. I couldn't do these things, so we needed Siew Cheh.

Eng Cheh used to do the washing and cleaning, but since Yong Cheh was tied up with Ma these days, Eng Cheh had taken over the cooking as well. She could only make simple things. She didn't know how to cook chicken curry, assam pedas or babi pongtey – all my favourite dishes – but at this time, we needed her as well.

For these reasons, I decided not to say anything about the jewellery until Ma got better. I knew I had to be strong to take care of Ming because he was getting heavy, so I tried to finish my food even if it was too dry or salty. I usually ate by myself these days, but the good thing was that I didn't have to worry about table manners. Ma was always telling me to eat in a more ladylike way and chew with my mouth closed. Now I could eat as loudly as I liked.

Papa had stopped going out to conduct business. He spent all day in his study with the door closed. Siew Cheh brought him his meals, and he ate in there by himself. I was relieved that he was not crying anymore. I knew because every day after dinner, I would tiptoe to his door and listen. I usually heard the radio broadcasting news about the war.

One evening, as I was stealthily approaching his study, the door suddenly opened. Papa was surprised to see me.

"Bee! Just the person I'm looking for!"

"Uh, yes?" I answered guiltily.

"I have good news for you," he said, looking pleased.

Papa told me that he had engaged a tutor for me. His name was Mr DeSouza, and he would be teaching me English, Maths and Science. The best part of all was that Janet, my best friend from St Mary's, would be joining the class. I had not seen her since the last day of school, and I was excited.

SEVEN

On the day of our first tuition class, Janet arrived early. I ran to open the door for her myself. We held hands and jumped up and down.

"I can't believe you're here!" I exclaimed.

"I can't believe I'm here too," she cried. "I thought I was going to die from boredom at home."

"I know! I've been so bored."

"Are you lonely now that Ying is dead?" she asked.

"Mmm," I mumbled.

I really didn't want to talk about Ying. Luckily, our tutor showed up just then. We were so surprised when we saw him. He was young, tall and good-looking – not what we had expected at all. I ran to the study to tell Papa. When Papa introduced us, Mr DeSouza shook hands with Janet and me, which made us giggle. Papa settled us at the round marble table in the dining room and left.

Mr DeSouza seemed a little nervous. "So, you're in Primary Four?" he asked us.

Janet spoke up before I could. "We started Primary Four, but after only a few weeks, a bomb dropped on our school and killed a bunch of people!"

Mr DeSouza was taken aback. He cleared his throat. "Yes, I heard. I'm so sorry about what happened to your school."

He looked at me when he said this, so I think he knew about Ying. He paused and seemed to be thinking of what to say next.

"I will be teaching you English, Maths and Science. I hope you like these subjects, but uh, we can also learn about anything you're interested in," he said. "I believe that education is about inquiry, so I encourage you to be curious. So please, ask me anything you like."

At this point, Siew Cheh came in with a tray of barley drinks. She looked shy and said "Sir" when she handed Mr DeSouza his cup.

"Thank you," he mumbled, and blushed! We sipped our drinks quietly. Then Janet raised her hand high as if we were in a classroom full of students.

"Yes, Janet?" Mr DeSouza said encouragingly.

"I'm curious, Mr DeSouza, what kind of Eurasian are you? I mean, are you English or Dutch, and mixed with what kind of Asian – Chinese, Malay, or Indian?"

Mr DeSouza choked on his barley. He coughed, and his face turned red. When he recovered, he said quietly, "Let's not have personal questions, please."

I didn't dare to look at Janet because I was afraid I would burst out laughing. I think she felt the same way because she kicked my foot under the table.

Mr DeSouza was a good teacher, and the two-hour lesson went by quickly. After he left, Janet and I went up to my room. I laid on my stomach on the bed, and Janet sat cross-legged on the floor.

"Oh my gosh, Bee! Where did your father find him?" she gushed.

"I expected a boring old man," I giggled.

"Me too! How old do you think he is?"

I raised my hand and said, "I'm curious, Mr DeSouza, how old are you?"

Janet made her voice deep and said, "Let's not have personal questions, please."

We burst out laughing.

Janet stuck her hand up and said, "I'm curious, Mr DeSouza, do you have a girlfriend?"

I put on my deepest voice and said, "Let's not have personal questions, please."

We squealed with laughter as we took turns asking all sorts of questions and imitating Mr DeSouza. I could hear the baby crying, probably because we had woken him up with all the noise we were making, but I didn't care. We laughed until our stomachs hurt.

Suddenly, I felt a sharp pain on the back of my leg. "Ow!" I yelped.

"What?" Janet asked, staring at me like I was crazy.

"I don't know! Can you see anything here?" I pointed to the painful spot.

She came over to take a look. "Wah, it's turning blue-black."

"Blue-black? Are you sure?" I asked, a chilling thought forming in my mind.

"Yes, what happened?"

"Er, maybe I banged it?"

"Banged it on what? Why did you suddenly scream like that?"

"Er ... maybe a ghost pinched me?" I laughed nervously.

"Bee Ling, you're very strange, you know?" Janet said, rolling her eyes.

I could still hear the baby crying. "Wait, I better go and

check on Ming," I said, and hurried out of the room.

I was sure I knew what had happened to my leg, but Janet would not have believed me. I remembered Ying's pinches well – the way they had felt and the blue-black marks they had left behind. Maybe Ying was angry that we were making so much noise, or maybe she wanted me to take care of the baby. Where in the world was Siew Cheh?

"I'm sorry, Ming Ming," I said as I lifted him from his cot.

"Waaah!" he yelled, his face scrunched up like an angry old man.

His diaper was soaking wet, so I put him back and went to look for Siew Cheh. I ran all over the house, but she was nowhere to be found.

Janet's chauffeur came to pick her up, so I decided to change Ming's diaper myself. I did what I had seen Siew Cheh do a million times. I spread the rubber changing mat on the table and laid Ming on it. Then I took off the wet diaper. It was disgusting! I shook powder all over Ming's bottom and his boy parts. I think he liked it because he made happy noises.

Siew Cheh had already folded a stack of clean diapers, so I took one and carefully slipped it under Ming's buttocks. Then came the hard part. I didn't know how to pin the diaper together. I tried putting one corner with another, but the diaper would not stay on. In the meantime, Ming had fallen asleep.

Finally, I decided to bunch all the cloth in the middle and pin everything together. There were many layers of cloth, and I struggled to push the big safety pin through. The pin started bending, and my fingers hurt, but I managed to fasten it just as Ming woke up crying. I felt proud of myself when I picked Ming up and the diaper stayed on him. But now he was wailing. I tried to rock him, but he kicked and screamed. Finally, Siew

Cheh ran in and took him from me.

"Oh Ming Ming, what's wrong?" she cooed as she rocked him, but he was inconsolable.

"Where were you?" I demanded.

"Sorry, I had a stomachache," she said, embarrassed.

Ming howled. His face had turned a dark shade of red.

"Hurry up and make his milk!" I ordered.

"Right away, Miss," Siew Cheh said agreeably and laid Ming in his cot. It was then she noticed his diaper, all bunched up in the middle.

"Did you change his diaper?" she asked, staring at me with a strange look on her face.

"Yes! I couldn't find you anywhere," I said accusingly.

She undid the safety pin, and the diaper fell open. We both gasped. There was blood on Ming's boy parts! I must have poked him with the safety pin! I felt terrible, but I blamed Siew Cheh.

"It's all your fault!" I yelled, tears stinging my eyes. "You're supposed to take care of him, not me. I hate you!"

Just then, Papa came into the room. He glared at me and said sternly, "Bee Ling, go to your room now."

I knew that I was in trouble because Papa always told me to treat the amahs respectfully. I went to my room, feeling angry. Why was I getting punished when I had been trying to help?

I was still sulking when I remembered what had happened to my leg earlier. I took a small mirror from my desk drawer and held it behind the painful spot. Sure enough, I saw a familiar blue-black mark.

Angrily, I yelled, "I hate you too, Ying!"

The desk drawer suddenly slammed shut. Startled, I jumped into bed and threw the blanket over my head. This was too unfair, I thought, as my heart thumped loudly in my chest.

EIGHT

Janet and I had tuition with Mr DeSouza three times a week. I looked forward to these days because firstly, Mr DeSouza was a really good teacher, and secondly, Janet and I always had so much fun after class.

Aside from his ban on personal questions, Mr DeSouza was true to his word and answered our questions about a lot of things. We learned that Japan was attacking Singapore and Malaya as part of a greater war that had begun in China in 1937. Singapore was part of the British Empire which was now at war in Europe. This made it difficult for Britain to defend her colonies in the Far East. For the first time, I started worrying that the British Army would not be able to protect us.

"What will happen to us if the Japanese capture Singapore?' I asked.

Mr DeSouza looked grim. "Well, they will become our new rulers. We will have to wait and see what rules they make for us."

"I heard that they are evil. They torture people and cut off their heads!" Janet said.

Mr DeSouza spoke sternly. "This is a scary time for everyone, not just children. We must be careful not to listen to hearsay."

Janet pouted because not only did Mr DeSouza criticise her for listening to rumours, he had also referred to us as children.

After class, Janet and I went up to my room. Janet sighed as she lay on my bed. "Don't you think Mr Dee looks even more handsome with his new haircut?" she asked.

She had started calling him "Mr Dee", which made him uncomfortable, but he did not ask her to stop.

"You're hopeless!" I giggled.

She laughed. "I wish I was old enough to be his girlfriend."

"We still have no idea how old he is," I reminded her.

"Let's have some personal questions, please!" she begged.

"Yes, please," I agreed.

"I have an idea!" She sat up excitedly. "Next lesson, we'll tell him that we're doing a project. We'll write down the names and ages of all the people we know, and we'll ask him to add his information to the list."

"But he's going to ask what the project is for," I said.

"We can say that we're keeping a record, in case people get killed by the Japanese."

My stomach tightened into a knot. "Do you think the Japanese will kill more people we know?"

Janet rolled her eyes. "For goodness' sake, Bee Ling, it's just an excuse for Mr Dee! Quick, get me a piece of paper!"

We never got to do our project because our next lesson with Mr DeSouza was cancelled. That morning, Papa instructed the amahs to bolt all the windows and doors. I knew it was serious because Ma, looking pale as a ghost, came downstairs with Yong Cheh's help. Papa asked everyone to sit at the dining table.

"This morning, the Japanese captured Bukit Timah Hill," Papa said gravely. "They cannot be stopped now. They are also coming in from Punggol. It won't be long before they reach us here in Katong."

Eng Cheh whimpered. The rest of us were silent. Singapore had fallen to the Japanese. What would happen to us now?

"Don't worry, we have food to last us for at least 6 months. By then, I expect that the British will reclaim Singapore," Papa said. "For now, I want everyone to stay inside the house. Do not open the door for anyone. Stay alert, and let me know if you see or hear anything unusual." Papa looked at each of us to make sure we understood.

"Papa, are we safe in here?" I asked.

Before he could answer, Ma spoke. "Yes, Bee, we are safe. God will protect us."

Her voice was surprisingly strong and gave me courage. Papa reached for her hand and squeezed it.

It was strangely quiet for the rest of the day. Our windows had metal grilles on the outside and wooden shutters on the inside. Once the shutters were closed, the house became dark and quiet as a tomb. Ma returned to bed. Papa went to his study, but this time, he left the door open. The amahs retreated to their rooms at the back of the house.

I had told Siew Cheh that I would look after Ming, so she had moved his cot into my room. When Ming woke up, I fed him the milk that Siew Cheh had prepared. Then I placed his head on my shoulder and patted his back until he burped twice. I put Ming on my bed and sat next to him. He lay on his back, gripping his tiny toes in his hands.

"Ming Ming, are you scared of the Japanese?" I asked him.

"Woh woh, wah woh!" Ming said. Then he stuck his toes in

his mouth.

"I guess you're not scared. That makes you the bravest person in this house," I told him.

Ming replied by sucking noisily on his toes. I took them out of his mouth and gave him a pacifier. Soon, he fell asleep. It was nice to watch him sleeping peacefully, with not a care in the world.

NINE

I woke up in the morning to an unfamiliar, rhythmic sound. Peering through the slats of my window shutters, I saw hundreds of soldiers marching down the road in front of our house. They wore green uniforms and carried guns. Fear gripped my chest as I realised that I was looking at the Japanese Imperial Army – they were the ones who had bombed my school and killed my sister!

I immediately ran downstairs. I found Papa on the telephone, looking grim. "Yes, I understand ... we'll be careful," he said.

Papa looked troubled as he hung up the telephone. Quietly, I followed him as he headed to the back of the house.

The amahs were huddled together at the kitchen table, whispering. They were surprised to see Papa and me.

"Sir?" Siew Cheh asked.

"I need you to prepare today's and tomorrow's meals and pack it all in the tingkat. Madam, Bee Ling, Ming Ming and all of you will go into the bomb shelter as soon as this is ready. Siew Cheh, make sure you have everything that Ming needs for two days," Papa said.

"Two days! Why, Papa?" I exclaimed, alarmed at the thought of being in that dark, stuffy hole for such a long time.

"Just to be safe, no need to worry," Papa said, but he looked anxious.

"Two days in there? What if I need to use the toilet?" I asked.

"Good point," Papa said. He turned to Eng Cheh. "Make sure to bring the chamber pots."

"Eee! So disgusting," I said, before I could stop myself.

I expected Papa to scold me, but his voice was gentle. "Bee, you're now the big sister of the family. You need to be strong and help everyone."

I couldn't be sure, but I thought that Papa had tears in his eyes, so I decided not to complain anymore.

Yong Cheh, in spite of her old age and heavy body, was a fast worker. With Eng Cheh's help, she soon prepared four tingkat of freshly cooked rice, tofu, fish, and eggs. Siew Cheh boiled water and filled three vacuum flasks for Ming's milk. She packed some clean baby clothes and diapers, then lined a big basket with blankets to make a bed for Ming.

For myself, I brought a pillow, a packet of lemon cream biscuits, and a book that Mr DeSouza had asked us to read – *Great Expectations* by Charles Dickens. I knew that Ying had a copy, but I also remembered how she had hated it when I borrowed her things. Nervously, I had gone into her room, grabbed the book and run out. I was glad that she didn't pinch me. I also asked Papa to give me lots of candles and matches because I was afraid of the dark.

We gathered our things and settled in the bomb shelter.

"Do you have everything you need?" Papa asked, looking at us from the small doorway.

"Yes, Sir. Don't worry, we'll take care of the family," Yong Cheh assured him.

"Thank you, Yong Cheh," Papa said.

Ma, who was sitting on a small mattress that Papa had brought in for her, called out, "Henry, please be careful!"

"I'll be fine, dear. Don't worry about me," he replied.

"Papa, please stay with us," I begged, hoping that he would change his mind.

"Bee, remember what we talked about?"

Earlier, Papa had come into my room and explained that Japanese soldiers were going into people's homes, especially nice houses like ours. He said they were only looking for things like clocks and radios, and not to worry. We would just wait in the bomb shelter until it was over. I had promised Papa that I would be brave, but now I regretted it. I bit my bottom lip and held back my tears.

"It's just for two days. I'll let you out when it's safe," he assured me.

I braced myself as Papa shut the door. Then I heard him dragging the big kitchen cupboard, and I knew that he was moving it in front of the door to conceal it.

TEN

In the dim candlelight, the small room seemed to have shrunk. I felt my chest tighten and worried that there wasn't enough air for all of us. I couldn't control myself and let out a sob. Siew Cheh put her arm around me and squeezed my shoulder.

"Don't worry, Bee. We'll take care of you," she said kindly.

I let her pull me close and cried softly on her shoulder as I had done in the past, when I had quarrelled with Ying or when Ma had scolded me.

The silence and darkness created the feeling that time stood still. Luckily, Papa had given me his old pocket watch, and this was the only thing that told us time was moving, one small tick at a time.

Siew Cheh sat next to me, while Ming slept on her other side. Across from us, Ma lay on the mattress against the wall. Yong Cheh and Eng Cheh crouched in a corner where they whispered together.

I lit a few extra candles so that I could read my book. *Great Expectations* transported me from the small, stuffy room to the cold, foggy marshes of England. I forgot my own problems and felt sorry for the orphan boy, Pip, who was bullied by his ill-tempered older sister.

I was glad whenever Ming woke up because I could help to feed him and play with him. When it was dinner time, the amahs waited for Ma and me to finish eating before they started. No one was hungry, except for Yong Cheh. The food made her even more talkative.

"You think this is hardship, Bee?" she asked cheerfully.

"We're like mice hiding in a dark hole," I pointed out.

"Do you know what it was like on the boat when I came from China? We were like chickens in a coop, all stuffed together – men and women, dead and alive."

"Dead?"

"Oh yah. Many people died along the way. Sometimes, they threw the bodies into the sea, other times, the corpses rotted right next to us. Aiyoh, the smell ah! People throwing up left and right, soiling themselves here and there –"

"Yong Cheh, I think that's enough," Ma said.

Unfortunately, that put an end to the stories.

Three round metal chamber pots had been placed at the far corner of the room, behind some boxes. I soon realised that whenever someone was using the chamber pot, everyone could hear it. I was embarrassed to go, but eventually, I couldn't bear it any longer. I told the amahs that they had to cover their ears until I finished. They laughed.

"Aiyoh! Bee, have you forgotten who changed your diapers and wiped your backside?" Yong Cheh cackled.

"But Bee is a young lady now," Siew Cheh said.

"That one?" Yong Cheh scoffed. "No lah, not like Ying."

"Can you just shut up and do as you're – ouch!" I jumped.

I knew that Ma was asleep, but I didn't know that Ying was listening! She had pinched me again, hard. I acted as if nothing had happened.

"Cover your ears until I come back, *please*," I instructed.

It was funny to see the three amahs squatting in a row, hands over their ears. I lit two more candles and carefully carried them over to the chamber pots. I set the candles on the ground and carefully lowered myself onto one of the small metal pots. I had to concentrate on my balance as I relieved myself. I wondered how Yong Cheh, who was so large, managed to do it.

Time passed slowly, but finally, we came to the end of the first day. I lay next to Ming's basket, waiting for sleep to come. I thought of the story I was reading. I imagined Estella, the beautiful girl that Pip was in love with. I wondered why she enjoyed insulting him so much. I mused about the strange Miss Havisham who always wore her old wedding dress. She seemed frightening. Soon, I fell asleep.

Loud noises woke me up. I heard glass shattering and what sounded like pots and pans clanging in the kitchen. Before I could react, Siew Cheh was squeezing my hand tightly. She put a finger to her lips. I covered my mouth with my hand to stop myself from crying out. What was going on outside? What was happening to Papa? We held our breath as we heard shouting. Suddenly, there was a deafening bang – a gunshot! All was quiet after that.

I could only imagine the worst. Slowly, our terrified silence turned into crying. During the commotion, Siew Cheh had pressed Ming to her chest to muffle his cries, but now his wails filled the room. One by one, we joined him – sniffling, whimpering, and finally, weeping.

I ran to the door and pounded it with my fists, calling, "Papa! Papa!"

There was no reply, and the door remained firmly shut.

ELEVEN

If time had crawled slowly the first day, the second day was torturously slow. We were gripped with the fear that something terrible had happened to Papa, and all we could do was to wait helplessly.

The bomb shelter had once been our garage, but the garage door had been nailed shut with wooden planks on the outside and lined with sandbags on the inside. Our only way out was through the small door in the kitchen wall, but Papa had blocked it with the heavy cupboard. We were now trapped inside our hiding place.

Ma seemed to have regained her strength. She carried Ming and paced up and down. She told me to pray and trust God. She said that Papa would let us out when the time was right.

"But Ma, the gunshot! What if Papa –"

"Si geena!" Yong Cheh scolded. "Your big mouth will bring bad luck!"

"Yong Cheh, please don't call Bee Ling that horrible name," Ma said, "and as Christians, we're not superstitious." She turned to me. "Bee, I know you're scared, but it's important to trust God."

"But –" I started to say.

"If you're afraid, say a prayer," Ma insisted.

"Well, can I pray for this candle to last forever? Because it's the last one!"

Everyone stared at me. Papa had given me a big box of candles. He said there would be enough, so I had used as many as I liked. I was shocked when I saw that I had burned through our stash. Our last candle was barely three inches long.

The amahs started rummaging through the baskets and boxes, looking for more candles, but came up empty-handed. Yong Cheh glared at me and started to scold, "Si –", but she glanced at Ma and bit her tongue.

I felt hot tears pricking my eyes. "It's not my fault! Papa said that he had given us plenty of candles!"

Ma sighed. I looked at Siew Cheh for support, but she wouldn't meet my gaze. Ma gave the amahs instructions to organise things so that we could find them in the dark – important things, such as Ming's milk. The amahs worked quickly.

My mind blocked out the activity around me as I focused on the last candle. I stared at the orange flame, thinking of the darkness that was waiting to take over. I had always been afraid of the dark – it was like a thick and heavy blanket that threatened to smother me.

I gazed at the flame until my eyes watered. Beads of wax slid down the sides of the candle. I thought of Papa's kind and handsome face. What if he had been captured or killed by Japanese soldiers?

The candle was growing shorter and shorter before my eyes. It would not be long before the light went out. I dreaded the moment so much that I found myself counting under my breath, "One, two, three, four ..."

I imagined that the candle was keeping time with my counting, burning down bit by bit with each number that I muttered under my breath.

"… ninety-five, ninety-six, ninety-seven …" The more I counted, the more my dread grew, but it had become a childish game, and I was strangely excited to find out what number I would reach when the flame finally died.

"… two hundred and twenty-two, two hundred and twenty-three …" It was still going. My heart pounded in my chest as the flame greedily gobbled up the wax.

The candle was now a small lump of wax with a flickering flame. "… three hundred and fifty-three, three hundred and fifty-four, three hundred and –" And the light went out. In that instant, I felt as if I had been swallowed up by a whale, just like the Sunday school story. There was nothing to do now but to sit in its deep, dark belly. I closed my eyes and breathed deeply, trying not to panic.

My mind went back to a stormy night a long time ago. A loud crash of thunder had woken me up. The wind was howling, and the rain was beating against the windows. I grabbed my bolster and ran to Ying's room, shaking her awake and climbing into bed with her. Terrified of the darkness and the noise from the storm, I started crying. Ying told me to close my eyes. Then she recited something that I had heard in Sunday school, "The Lord is my Shepherd, I shall not want …"

I knew one part quite well because Ying had asked me to repeat it after her. Crouching in the dark now, I said it under my breath, "I will fear no evil, for You are with me … You are with me." I knew that "You" in the poem meant God, but when I said it, I thought of Ying. I suddenly remembered that she was here with me!

"Ying? Ying!" I whispered into the darkness.

I jumped when she touched my face. It was as if a feather had lightly brushed my cheek, but I knew it was her.

"Say sorry," her voice said in my ear.

"What?" I asked.

"Say sorry."

I heard Ying so clearly. Could anyone else hear her?

"But it's not my – ouch! Can you stop doing that?" I hissed, rubbing my arm. It was the same old, bossy Ying!

Deep inside, I knew that it was my fault for using too many candles, but I didn't want to admit it. Realising that I had no choice, I announced to the pitch-black room, "I'm sorry about the candles. It's my fault, and I'm sorry."

"Si geena," Yong Cheh muttered from somewhere in the darkness.

Ma sounded pleased. "It's all right, Bee. I'm proud of you for admitting your mistake."

In the next moment, a gush of wind swept through the darkness, roaring in our ears, pulling our hair and clothes in its path, and flinging the kitchen door wide open.

TWELVE

Our house had been looted. Our China vases, table lamps, clocks and radios were missing. Our rosewood tables and chairs, in-laid with mother-of-pearl, were stolen. Even our silk curtains were snatched from the rails. Our house had been ransacked, and the only things left behind were broken and scattered on the ground. When Ma saw the house like this, she fainted.

Anxious about Papa, I ran into every room, upstairs and downstairs, shouting, "Papa! Papa!" I dashed back and forth, looking into cupboards, behind doors, and even under the beds. When it became clear that Papa was not in the house, even though I knew I was not supposed to, I ran out the front door.

Outside, the street was empty, and there was a burning smell in the air. I hurried until I came to the main road, and there I was met with a chilling sight. The road was full of soldiers, both British and Japanese. The Japanese troops carried guns, but the British soldiers were holding brooms and sweeping the road! I couldn't believe my eyes. The British soldiers who had always looked so strong and smart in their uniforms – how could they be doing such a demeaning task? Then I noticed the white flags with the red sunrays hanging from the lorries. My heart clenched even though I already knew – Singapore had fallen to the Japanese.

On both sides of the road, local men were quietly staring at the strange scene. A lorry full of British soldiers started pulling away. To my surprise, I heard the soldiers singing. It was a song I recognised from Ma's records:

Wish me luck as you wave me goodbye
Cheerio, here I go, on my way …

I knew that these soldiers were captured, and their bravery at this moment brought tears to my eyes. Suddenly, I felt a sharp tug on my sleeve. I turned, but no one was there. This was what Ying used to do to get my attention. I decided to head home before she pinched me.

As I ran back down the street, I saw Siew Cheh hurrying towards me.

"Bee! What are you doing here? We were so scared when we couldn't find you!"

"I was looking for Papa," I explained.

"We will find your Pa, but it's not safe out here. Quick, let's go home!"

My bedroom had also been looted. My collection of dolls with porcelain faces was missing. My nice dresses, including the blue one I had worn last Christmas, were gone. Thankfully, my books were not taken, but they were strewn on the ground and stamped with black shoe prints. I picked them up and carefully cleaned them with a piece of torn clothing before putting them back on the shelves.

Under the bed, I found an old teddy bear. There were bits

of string around its neck, where a little necklace used to be, and one of its ears was torn, but I was glad to see it. I sat on the bed and hugged the soft, furry bear. I could not stop my tears from falling. I realised that what Ying had said about me was true. I was childish. I had thought that I was so grown up after my tenth birthday, but now I felt small and useless.

A draught of cool air blew through the room. I shivered and hugged the bear tighter. I felt the mattress being pressed down next to me. I couldn't see her, but I knew that Ying was sitting beside me.

"They can take everything, I don't care. I just want Papa," I told her.

Ying's reply was a cool, gentle touch on my shoulder. Just like before, it comforted me.

The amahs worked tirelessly to clean up the mess. They picked everything up, swept the floors, and wiped the teak floorboards with vinegar until they shone again. Then they bathed Ma and the baby, and put them both to bed. They also cooked dinner for me. The hot porridge and crispy salted fish tasted delicious. Thankfully, we had stored our food in the bomb shelter.

After dinner, Siew Cheh told me that we should telephone Papa's friends for help. We went into Papa's study and managed to find his old address book. I flipped through the pages until I saw a familiar name: Charles Harrison. He was Katie's dad. I dialled the number and heard a ringing tone, but no one picked up. Then I remembered Papa saying that British citizens had left Singapore. I looked through the address book again, and my heart leapt when I saw the name Phillip DeSouza. I dialled the phone number nervously.

Mr DeSouza's warm, familiar voice answered on the third

ring. I immediately launched into my story. "Mr DeSouza, it's Bee Ling. My Papa is gone! We were hiding in the bomb shelter, and there were noises and gunshots and – and now he's missing! Please help find my Papa!"

"I'm so sorry to hear this, Bee Ling," he said, "Calm down, I will do everything I can to help."

"Thank you, Mr DeSouza."

"I will make enquiries first thing tomorrow. For now, try not to worry and get a good night's sleep. Is there anything else?"

I didn't want our conversation to end, so I said, "I read *Great Expectations*. I mean, I haven't finished it yet, but I read quite a lot."

"I'm glad to hear that. What do you think of it?"

"Well, I'm happy for Pip that he's become a gentleman in London, but I don't like how he's mean to Joe. Joe was nice to Pip and took care of him."

"It sounds like you have an excellent understanding of the story. Let's discuss more in our next lesson."

"We're still having lessons?" I asked, my heart leaping with joy.

"The coming days will be chaotic, but I expect that things will eventually settle down, and we can continue with our lessons. Now you go on to bed. I will let you know when I find out about your Pa."

"Thank you," I said gratefully.

"No need to thank me, Bee Ling. Goodnight."

"Goodnight, Mr DeSouza."

I returned the phone to the cradle, feeling better. Siew Cheh had been listening to the whole conversation by pressing her ear against the other side of the earpiece. Now she turned to me and smiled. "Well done, Bee!" she said.

I found myself smiling back at her. At the time, neither of us suspected the sacrifice that would be needed to bring Papa home.

THIRTEEN

The morning after we came out of the bomb shelter, I woke up to Ma's raised voice. She was usually soft-spoken, so I was alarmed to hear her sounding shrill and upset. Panicked, I jumped out of bed and ran downstairs.

I found Ma and the three amahs in the back garden, gathered around the mango tree. Ma was livid. "We are a Christian family! I will not permit you to bring these – these pagan things into our home!" she fumed.

I saw what Ma was pointing at. A small vase of joss sticks, some frangipani flowers, and a plate of black watermelon seeds were arranged under the tree. Eng Cheh nervously studied her feet, and Siew Cheh looked worried, but Yong Cheh bravely faced Ma.

"Mam, it's for your daughter," she said.

"Bee Ling?" Ma asked, confused.

"No, Mam, it's for Ying."

Ma was outraged. Her lips trembled as she said, "How dare you – you disrespect her memory like this! My Ying was a good Catholic girl."

"Yes, Mam, but Ying's spirit is not at rest," Yong Cheh answered. "She is stuck here – in this house."

Eng Cheh let out a nervous squeak which, for a fleeting moment, I thought had come from my own heart! Ma swayed on her feet, and everyone rushed forward to catch her. She steadied herself and glared.

"Yong Cheh, you're too much!"

Yong Cheh shook her head calmly. "Forgive me, Mam, but I'm telling the truth. If you don't believe me, you can ask this si – Bee Ling."

Ma turned to me with her eyes narrowed. My stomach tightened. I knew that I would get into trouble if I told her about Ying.

Yong Cheh's eyes bored into mine. "When we were in the bomb shelter, I heard you talking to Ying. All the hair on my arms stood up, and wah, that wind! Ying opened the door for us, didn't she?" she demanded.

I looked away nervously, annoyed that nothing slipped by Yong Cheh, not even in the dark.

"Nonsense! Don't you put these silly ideas into Bee's head," Ma chided.

Yong Cheh took a step towards me and warned, "Bee Ling, you better explain!"

Desperate, I looked at Siew Cheh for help.

"Bee is scared of the dark. I'm sure she was just praying, right, Bee?" Siew Cheh said.

Yong Cheh exploded with rage. "Siew Cheh, no one asked you to speak, so keep your mouth shut! I'm asking the si geena," she barked.

But now I knew what the correct answer would be. "I was frightened, so I prayed for everyone, including Ying," I said.

Ma's expression softened. "That was clever, Bee. Remember, if you're scared, you can ask Saint Francis for courage."

But Yong Cheh would not give up. "I may be old, but I'm not mad! Never mind what this si geena says. Tell me, Mam, how could the door open when the kitchen cupboard was blocking it?"

"I'm sure that Henry moved the cupboard. You can ask him when he comes home. Yong Cheh, I insist that you stop all this nonsense and remove these pagan things at once. This is a Christian home."

With that, she turned and walked towards the house in her elegant way, her red khakiak lightly clicking on the stone path through the garden. I quickly followed in my bare feet, afraid that Yong Cheh would interrogate me again.

FOURTEEN

All day long, I waited for the phone to ring. I was anxious to hear Mr DeSouza's news about Papa. I tried to continue reading *Great Expectations*, but I could not concentrate. I paced back and forth with Ming in my arms, long after he had fallen asleep.

In the late evening, the phone rang. I snatched it up on the second ring.

"Mr DeSouza?" I asked, gripping the phone tightly.

"Hello, Bee Ling. Sorry I couldn't call earlier. I –"

"Did you find Papa?"

"Yes, I –"

My heart leapt. "Where's Papa? Is he all right?"

"He's fine ... Can I speak to your mother?" he asked.

Ma was under the impression that Papa had gone out to take care of some business. She did not suspect that he was in any kind of danger. I feared that any bad news of Papa would be too much for her heart.

"Ma has a very weak heart, Mr DeSouza. Please, tell me where Papa is."

"Bee Ling, it's serious. I have to speak to an adult," he insisted.

Siew Cheh had joined me at the phone, so I said, "Please

talk to Siew Cheh. Hold on."

She took my place in front of the telephone. "Hello, Mr DeSouza. This is Siew Cheh speaking," she said.

I pressed my ear against the other side of the earpiece.

"Hello, Siew Cheh. Please, er, call me Phillip. I have information about Mr Song. The good news is that he is alive. Unfortunately, he's been arrested by the Kempeitai, the Japanese military police. He's at the YMCA building in Stamford Road. It's their headquarters now."

Siew Cheh's eyes widened and mirrored my fear. "Do you know why they arrested Mr Song?" she asked.

"The Japanese are arresting a lot of people," he replied. "They are targeting those suspected of spying for China or Britain. Mr Song had many British friends. I think that's why they took him."

I gasped. Papa was suspected of being a spy!

"Is there anything you can do, Mr De – Mr Phillip?" Siew Cheh asked.

"To be honest, it's a terrible time. The Japanese are …" Siew Cheh turned away from me, and I could not hear what Mr DeSouza said next.

"I understand, Mr Phillip, thank you," Siew Cheh said, and hung up.

"Does this mean that Papa is never coming back?" I asked tearfully.

"No, he did not say that. It's good news – your Pa is alive, Bee."

"But when can he come home?"

"I'm afraid we will have to wait and hope for the best."

It was a warm night, and I could not fall asleep. I lay in bed thinking about Papa. I thought of what Janet had said about the Japanese. What if they cut off Papa's head? My heart started pounding, and I remembered Ma's advice. For the first time in a long while, I knelt beside my bed and clasped my hands together.

"Saint Francis, I pray for courage," I said aloud. I recalled learning in Chapel that Saint Jude was the Saint of Lost Causes, so I added, "Saint Jude, please help Mr DeSouza to save Papa. Thank you, I mean, Amen."

Ying would approve of my prayer, I thought. As Ma said, Ying had been a good Catholic girl. She used to read the bible with Ma. They had invited me to join them, but I found it boring.

I thought of the amahs' offering for Ying under the mango tree. I supposed that if I were a ghost, I would enjoy receiving gifts. Ying's favourite sweets were caramel toffees, but our chocolates and nice candies had been stolen. I checked my desk drawers. Before the looting, they were full of pencils, rubbers and ribbons. Now I could only find a few broken pencils and a bookmark of the Virgin Mary. I knew that Ying would like the bookmark.

All of a sudden, I remembered the hairpin! Clutching my mattress with both hands, I lifted it as high as I could and was delighted to see my old school sock sitting on the baseboard. Still gripping the mattress, I stuck out one foot and grabbed the sock with my toes. My heart skipped as I held the sock in my hand. Carefully, I tilted it, and the gold hairpin with red rubies slid out. I was overjoyed that the looters had missed such a precious thing!

The hairpin was Ma's gift to Ying on her twelfth birthday,

and Ying had loved it more than anything. She was not allowed to wear it to school, so she had worn it to church and on special occasions, like the time we had dinner at Raffles Hotel with Papa's friends.

We had all dressed up that evening – Ma in her best silk cheongsam, Ying and I in newly tailored dresses, and Papa in a smart white suit. Siew Cheh had carefully curled Ying's hair before fixing the hairpin in place. The red rubies sparkled against Ying's glossy black hair. The amahs fluttered around her, gushing compliments. Ma said that Ying looked like a young lady. Siew Cheh offered to curl my hair, but I told her not to bother. I was sure that next to Ying, no one would even notice me.

At the hotel, we sat in a large dining room with white tablecloths and sparkling silverware. The high ceiling was lined with electric fans, and an elegantly dressed lady played the piano. During the meal, Ying kept touching her hairpin to make sure that it hadn't fallen off. Everyone said that she was very pretty. I had an itchy rash from my new dress, and on the way home, Ma scolded me for scratching "like a little monkey".

A few days after the dinner at Raffles Hotel, Ying and I had a big fight. Not surprisingly, Ma took Ying's side and punished me, so out of revenge, I stole Ying's hairpin and put it under my mattress. Ying cried for days, but I refused to admit that I had taken it. In the end, Ma took Ying to the jewellery shop at Alkaff Arcade and bought her not only another hairpin with red rubies but a matching necklace as well. Ying showed off her jewellery when she came home, and the amahs oohed and ahhed like silly old monkeys. That was why I never returned this hairpin to her.

Now I laid a handkerchief on the windowsill. Carefully, I

arranged the beautiful hair ornament and the bookmark of the Virgin Mary on the square of white cloth. The rubies glittered in the moonlight. It was my offering to Ying. I wanted to thank her for saving us, and I hoped that she liked it.

FIFTEEN

Something was happening outside. Through our boarded-up windows and bolted doors, I could hear people making announcements in various Chinese dialects with loudhailers. I could not understand what they were saying because I only knew a handful of Hokkien words. Siew Cheh explained that all Chinese men had to report for inspection by the Japanese Army. I wondered if the Kempeitai was "inspecting" Papa, and if he could come home after that. This was one of the times when I wished we had more family.

Ying and I always thought it was sad that we had no extended family. Unlike our friends, we had no grandparents, aunts, uncles or cousins. We felt left out when our friends talked about large family gatherings on Chinese New Year. At our own reunion dinners, there would only be Papa, Ma, Ying, me and our three amahs. The reunion dinner was the only time the amahs sat at the dinner table and ate with us.

A few years ago, after Ying's repeated begging, Ma had told us about Papa's family. My grandfather, Song Boon Hock, had been a first-generation immigrant from China. He had arrived in Singapore in the late 1800s and worked as a coolie on the docks, carrying heavy sacks between the ships and godowns.

He worked hard and avoided the opium and gambling dens. With his hard-earned savings, he started a small business with some friends.

My grandfather was smart, and he quickly became a successful businessman. He learned to speak English and Malay. He cut off his long pigtail and started wearing Western suits. Then he found the best matchmaker in town and married my grandmother, a beautiful Peranakan-Chinese girl named Sock Neo.

My father, Henry Song Teck Kin, was born soon after the marriage. A clever boy who was walking and talking by the time he was a year old, he was his parents' pride and joy. From the moment he was born, Papa was waited on hand-and-foot by amahs. Yong Cheh, who was just a young girl then, was among these servants.

Unfortunately, my grandmother could not bear another child. She consulted many sinseh and tried all sorts of herbal concoctions, but to no avail. Unlike his marriage, my grandfather's business ventures were fruitful. He bought a piece of land on Wilkie Terrace and built a mansion with five bedrooms. Complaining that his big house was empty, he took two more wives, both Peranakan women. My grandfather asked his first wife, my grandmother, to run the household as the matriarch of the family. Ma said that this had been common practice among wealthy Peranakan families, but my grandmother refused to accept it. She did not acknowledge the other wives and never spoke to my grandfather again.

The house was soon filled with my grandfather's children. My grandmother retreated to back of the house with her only son and two of her amahs – Yong Cheh and Eng Cheh.

When Papa was ten years old, my grandmother drank the

poison from the fruit of the pom pom tree in the back garden. Yong Cheh found her one morning, eyes wide-open and foam in her mouth.

Papa blamed his father. Like his mother, he rejected the other wives and their children. After my grandfather passed away, Papa left the big house and never saw any of the other family members again.

Ma never spoke about her own family, and even Ying did not dare to ask her about it. What I know, I learned from Siew Cheh, who had heard it from Yong Cheh, so I'm not sure how much of it is true. They said that Ma was born into a well-to-do family. She was the eldest of several children, both boys and girls. When Ma was fourteen, her family was struck by scarlet fever. The terrible disease claimed her parents as well as all her siblings. Ma survived, but the illness permanently weakened her heart.

Ma's relatives seized control of her family's fortune. They wanted to get rid of Ma, so as soon as she recovered, they arranged for her to be married. The night before her wedding, Ma put on five layers of clothing, climbed out of her bedroom window, and ran to a Catholic church for help. The kindhearted English sisters took her in and named her Ruth. Ma lived in the church orphanage where she taught the younger children to read and write. She also continued her own education with the sisters. When Ma was sixteen, she met Papa at Mass and they fell in love. They were married a year later.

This was why we also didn't have any extended family on Ma's side. All we had was our little family, and I was afraid that we were about to lose it.

SIXTEEN

It started at noon – a rapid *tat-tat-tat-tat-tat* in the distance. I wondered what it could be. I finished my watery porridge with pickled vegetables and went upstairs to my room. I opened the shutters a tiny bit and peered out. I could not be sure, but the sound seemed to be coming from the beach nearby.

A lorry with white and red Japanese flags rumbled past, and I was able to get a good look at it. The bed of the lorry was packed with people. I could see their faces as they passed under my window. I noticed that they were all Chinese men. They looked grim, and some were even crying. Where were they being taken, I wondered, and could Papa be among them? I was praying for Papa every night, but there was still no news from Mr DeSouza.

I heard Ming crying and went to his room. I checked his diaper, but it was dry. I guessed that he must be hungry. I had become good at carrying Ming, so I gave him a pacifier and took him downstairs.

In the kitchen, I found the amahs huddled together, whispering. They did not notice me. I listened carefully, but could only catch snippets of their conversation. "Hundreds … on the beach … no mercy …"

Without warning, Ming spat out his pacifier and let out a lusty wail. The amahs jumped. When they turned around, I was surprised to see that they were in tears.

"What's wrong? Is it Papa?" I asked anxiously.

"No, Bee, it's not your Pa," Siew Cheh answered as she took Ming from me.

"What are you all talking about?"

"Better you don't know," Yong Cheh said gruffly.

Eng Cheh nodded in agreement.

"Why? What is it? Tell me!"

"Si geena," Yong Cheh scolded, but her heart was not in it. She wiped her eyes with her handkerchief and blew her nose loudly.

When Siew Cheh finished making Ming's milk, I followed her out of the kitchen. She gave Ming his bottle in the dining room.

Tat-tat-tat-tat-tat. That sound again.

"What's that?" I asked.

"Yong Cheh is right, better you don't know," Siew Cheh said gently.

"You mean the sound? Is that what you were talking about?"

She nodded.

"What's happening?"

But Siew Cheh refused to tell me.

I went back to my room and kept watch at the window. I was determined to find out what was going on. It was a hot, cloudless day. There was no breeze or any sign of birds. Whatever was making that sound seemed to be scaring everything away.

Another military vehicle passed under my window. Just like the ones before, the back of the lorry was crammed with Chinese men. I watched it continue to the end of the street and slow down as it started to turn. Suddenly, a couple of men leapt out. They fell onto the road but quickly got to their feet and were running away. With a squeal of tires, the lorry jerked to a stop, and then everyone was jumping out and running off in all directions. Japanese soldiers emerged from the vehicle and pointed their guns. *Tat-tat-tat-tat-tat, tat-tat-tat-tat-tat.*

Immediately, I realised what I had been hearing all day, but in that same moment, I was flung back from the window onto my bed. I struggled to get up, but an invisible weight held me down. There was loud banging on our front door downstairs. It must be the men from the lorry! I wanted to open the door so that they could escape from the soldiers and their guns, but I couldn't move, and my feet felt cold as ice.

I lay on my bed helplessly, listening to the commotion outside as my thoughts raced. Japanese soldiers were shooting people on our street, perhaps even on our doorstep. From the sounds I had heard, they had been firing their guns all day. The amahs had mentioned the beach. I thought of the lorries I had seen, packed with men, all heading towards the beach. Were the men being taken there to be shot? What about Papa? Panicked, I struggled against the force holding me down.

"Papa! Papa!" I screamed.

"He's alive."

Ying was standing at the foot of my bed. Her almond-shaped eyes locked with mine. She gave me a smile that reassured me that Papa was okay. I had never seen her so close up since she had passed away. Her Head Girl uniform was neat and spotless, the gold pin glinting on the red tie. The sight of her calmed me. After a while, she faded into the air, and the weight lifted from me.

Military vehicles and soldiers flooded our street. There was a lot of shouting and banging. Ma came out of her room to find out what was happening.

"Mam, some men escaped! The Japanese soldiers are searching house-to-house. You must go in the bomb shelter with the children," Yong Cheh said. "Quick, before they come!"

"Thank you, Yong Cheh, we'll do that. Come on, Bee!" Ma said.

"Siew Cheh should go with you too," Yong Cheh suggested, "she's a young woman."

"Yes, of course," Ma said.

"Why can't we all hide together?" I asked.

"It will look suspicious if the house is empty. Eng Cheh and I will take care of things out here," Yong Cheh answered.

Eng Cheh looked frightened, but she nodded in agreement.

"Will you be safe?" I asked.

"Aiyoh, we're so old already," Yong Cheh replied as she hustled us towards the kitchen.

The amahs moved the kitchen cupboard to reveal the familiar door. With a shudder, I thought of what had happened the last time. Ma went into the shelter first, followed by Siew Cheh with Ming in her arms. I took a deep breath and stepped into the dark room after them.

Siew Cheh squeezed my shoulder. "Don't worry, Bee, it won't be long this time," she said.

Yong Cheh and Eng Cheh peered at us through the doorway.

"We'll let you out as soon as the soldiers are gone," Yong Cheh assured us.

"Be careful," I said.

Yong Cheh gave me a funny look. "Just worry about yourself," she said, but her voice was gentle.

She closed the door, and I heard them moving the cupboard. Once again, I found myself in total darkness. My heart thumped in my chest. "I can do this," I told myself and closed my eyes.

Next to me, Siew Cheh hummed softly and rocked Ming. I knew he was awake because I could hear him sucking on his pacifier. I concentrated on that little wet sound, and in my mind, I could see Ming's chubby cheeks moving up and down as his mouth clamped onto the pacifier. My fear began to melt away, and before I knew it, I dozed off.

It seemed like only moments later that Siew Cheh was tapping my shoulder. I opened my eyes to see light streaming in from the narrow doorway. I never thought I would be so thrilled to see Yong Cheh's face!

Once we stepped out of the bomb shelter, Yong Cheh excitedly filled us in on the soldiers' visit.

"There were two young men, very skinny, very tanned, both carrying guns," she said.

Eng Cheh nodded, patting her chest.

"They came in and looked everywhere, even opened all the cupboards," Yong Cheh continued. "Then they went upstairs, and suddenly, we heard them screaming! They ran down like a ghost was chasing them and went straight out the front door. Didn't even look back."

"No look back," Eng Cheh agreed.

"What happened?" Ma asked.

"Don't know. We came to let you out as soon as they left," Yong Cheh said.

Curiously, we all went upstairs to investigate but could not see any explanation for the soldiers' alarm.

"Are you sure they were screaming?" Ma asked.

"Mam, we may be old, but we're not senile," Yong Cheh replied crossly.

"Huh," Ma huffed.

"Strange," Siew Cheh mused.

"You should have seen their faces. They looked like they saw a ghost," Yong Cheh said, giving me a pointed look.

I bravely met her gaze and said, "But there's no such thing as ghosts, right, Ma?"

"Of course not! Just silly superstitions," Ma answered, just as I knew she would.

"Only your Saints are real, right, Mam?" Yong Cheh scoffed.

Ma's eyebrows shot up. "Yong Cheh, are you being insolent?"

"Of course not, Mam. Come, let me take you to your room," Yong Cheh said sweetly.

I watched Yong Cheh leading Ma away, wishing that I knew what Ying had done to frighten the soldiers so much.

SEVENTEEN

In the days that followed the incident on our street, I continued to hear the sound of guns firing from the beach. I stayed away from my window. I did not want to see the lorries full of men who were being taken to be shot and killed. I had nightmares where I saw Papa among them.

In one of these, I called to him from my window, "Papa! Papa!" He looked up at me and waved. As the lorry drove away, I continued yelling until I woke myself up. I looked around the dark room in confusion, my mind still filled with the image of Papa. The window shutters were slightly open, and a light breeze lifted the curtains. In the moonlight, I saw the glitter of Ying's hairpin on the windowsill. It reminded me of her assurance that Papa was alive and gave me much comfort.

I could not fall back to sleep, and my mind drifted to something that had happened in school last year. Our PE teacher, Sister Helen, had put me in charge of the sports equipment and given me a key to the equipment room. Unlike Ying, I was hardly ever put in charge of things, and I was proud to have been entrusted with this duty.

One day, I was in a desperate panic because I could not find my key. I had always kept it in a little pocket in my book bag, but this time, it wasn't there. I emptied out the whole bag and still could not find it. While everyone was changing into their PE attire, I ran to Ying's classroom on the third floor. The bell for the next class had not yet rung, and she immediately came out to me.

"What's wrong?"

"I lost my PE key!"

"Don't worry, Sister Helen should have a spare."

"I know, but I don't want to tell her that I lost it."

"She looks fierce, but she's actually quite nice."

"I'm sure she won't let me be in charge anymore," I said, blinking away my tears.

Ying paused for a moment. "Okay, wait here."

She went back to her classroom and soon returned with a key. "Come on!" Ying said, running off.

I followed her to the equipment room for the Primary Six girls, and she opened it. We grabbed the badminton rackets and shuttlecocks and went down to the field. I was nervous about what Sister Helen would say when she saw Ying, but she broke into a big smile.

"Ying Ying! What are you doing here?" she asked in a friendly voice.

"Good morning, Sister Helen," Ying said politely. "I hope you don't mind using our rackets today. I'm sorry I took Bee Ling's key by mistake, and I'm afraid I've lost it."

"Don't worry, I'll give her another one," Sister Helen said. "Make you sure you return everything upstairs, Bee Ling."

"Yes, Sister," I answered, feeling relieved.

"Thank you, Sister, and sorry for the trouble," Ying said.

As she ran back towards the school building, I couldn't help noticing how everyone was staring at her.

"So graceful," someone remarked.

"Her legs are so long," another gushed.

"So pretty, the way her hair moves."

I usually hated the attention that Ying got from my friends, but since she had come to my rescue, I didn't mind it as much on this occasion.

There were other times when Ying had come to my help, but I had never given them much thought before. It struck me that even though Ying had passed away, she continued to help me. Is that why she was still around?

EIGHTEEN

Mr DeSouza paid us a surprise visit. I had seen him for class only a few short weeks ago, but so much had changed since then. I wanted to give him a hug, but we politely shook hands instead. He explained that the Japanese Administration had given him a pass that allowed him to move about freely. The Japanese were mainly targeting Chinese men, and as a Eurasian, he was not under suspicion. He wanted to speak with me and Siew Cheh. We went to the dining room where we usually had class.

"I spoke to someone who can help your father. His name is Shinozaki."

"A Japanese?" I asked fearfully.

"Yes, a kindhearted Japanese official."

I held my breath, waiting for him to continue.

He turned to Siew Cheh. "Mr Shinozaki is negotiating with the Kempeitai for Mr Song's release. He said there are demands."

"What kind of demands?" Siew Cheh asked.

Mr DeSouza shifted uncomfortably and cleared his throat. "In exchange for Mr Song, they want an amah for their commanding officer."

For as long as I could remember, Yong Cheh, Eng Cheh and Siew Cheh had always been around. They were always in the background, taking care of our family. When we were hungry, food was already on the table, warm and waiting for us. We wore clothes that were clean and crisply ironed, slept on sheets that were smooth and stiff with starch, and walked on floors rubbed with vinegar until they shone and squeaked under our bare feet. I had taken all these things for granted.

In their white and black uniforms, with their hair oiled and neatly combed into buns, amahs all over Singapore looked the same. Maybe because of this, I didn't think of them as people who had their own lives, but merely as servants who cooked, cleaned and did our bidding. I would soon discover that I was wrong. It was only after I learned the amahs' stories that I would understand what happened that day.

Yong Cheh was born in Canton, China. Her parents were farmers. She spent her childhood working alongside her parents and two older brothers, growing yam, soya bean and a variety of vegetables. As hard as they worked, there was not enough money for them to live on. Yong Cheh's parents planned for her to work in a silk factory when she turned thirteen, but the factories in their village began shutting down, and many people lost their jobs.

On her thirteenth birthday, Yong Cheh's mother made her a hardboiled egg, dyed bright red, as well as a bowl of rice noodles in a special meat broth. Her father gave her a generous ang pow. He explained that the money was for her new life in the Nanyang. Yong Cheh's parents had decided to send her to the thriving British settlement of Singapore, where she could earn money as a domestic servant and lead an independent life. Yong Cheh knew that her parents had her best interests at heart, but she could not stop the tears that flowed into her noodles as she ate it. When she finished the bowl of noodles, she cracked her precious birthday egg and peeled its red shell. The pain in her chest made her feel as if she was peeling her own heart.

Early one morning, Yong Cheh's brothers and parents walked her down to the dock where a ship waited to take her away. The usually boisterous family was quiet. Yong Cheh put on a brave face and boarded the vessel.

From the deck of the ship, she watched her family standing on the shore, a tiny cluster within a large crowd. Already, they seemed a lifetime removed from her. Her heart clenched like a fist in her chest. When the boat began to pull away, everyone on the shore began to wave. She kept her eyes on her family and did not dare to blink, in case she could not find them in the crowd again. She watched and waved, until eventually, there was only the sea and sky.

After an arduous journey across the South China Sea, Yong Cheh arrived in Singapore. An agent brought her to a coolie fong. It was a place for amahs – Chinese women who dedicated their lives to being domestic servants. The amahs formed a sisterhood, and Yong Cheh was inducted through a formal ceremony where an elder amah oiled her hair and combed it into a tight bun.

Even though she was young, Yong Cheh was strong and stout – qualities that were prized in amahs. She was soon hired by my grandmother who liked her cheerful and chatty nature and personally taught her how to cook. Yong Cheh was a fast learner who mastered the art of balancing the flavours of cinnamon, clove and star anise. She knew the difference between white, yellow and blue ginger, and how to use each of them. With her strong arms, she could grind rempah on the mortar and pestle faster than anyone. Impressed with her, my grandmother assigned Yong Cheh the most important job in the household – taking care of her first child who would soon be born.

On her days off, Yong Cheh would visit the coolie fong to meet with other amahs. It was during one of these visits that Yong Cheh and Eng Cheh first met. Thin, quiet and timid, Eng Cheh was the opposite of Yong Cheh. Her long, droopy eyes made her look either sad or sleepy. On the day they had met, Eng Cheh had rushed into the coolie fong distraught, her hair disheveled and her white blouse torn. After a great amount of coaxing, Yong Cheh managed to get her story out of her.

Eng Cheh worked for a bad-tempered woman who scolded and beat her when she did not do her job well. On this day, Eng Cheh had accidentally poured bleach on a set of red bedsheets. When her employer saw this, she took off one of her khakiak to beat Eng Cheh with it. Terrified, Eng Cheh ran around as the woman grabbed her hair and clothes, swinging the wooden clog at her. This took place in the wash area where the cement floor was slippery with water and detergent. The irate woman slipped and fell on her face.

When Eng Cheh saw the blood dripping from the woman's mouth, she dashed out of the house and didn't stop running until she reached the coolie fong. Once inside, she cried uncontrollably, frightened that she had lost her job and would be arrested for her employer's injuries.

Yong Cheh's heart went out to this pitiful creature. She convinced my grandmother to employ Eng Cheh and took it upon herself to train her. In time, Eng Cheh became a competent amah. The two complemented each other with their different personalities and became good friends. Many years later, when Papa left the big house, Yong Cheh and Eng Cheh followed him.

When Mr DeSouza delivered the news that the Kempeitai wanted an amah in exchange for Papa, it erupted in the biggest quarrel that our three amahs ever had. Each of them wanted to go to the Japanese in order to save the others.

Yong Cheh said that she had taken care of Papa since he was born, so it was her duty to save him. Eng Cheh, who had never disagreed with Yong Cheh before, protested this time. She insisted that she was indebted to Yong Cheh and should go instead. Siew Cheh argued that as she was the youngest, she would be able to tolerate hardship best, but the others countered that it would be suicide for any young woman to go to the Japanese.

I watched in amazement as they went on arguing passionately. As the matter could not be resolved, Yong Cheh suggested asking Ma to make the decision.

"But Ma doesn't know that the Kempeitai has taken Papa. She still thinks that he's coming home soon," I reminded them.

"Bee is right. We have to think of her heart," Siew Cheh said.

"Well, in that case, we'll let this one decide." Yong Cheh pointed at me.

"Me? No way, I'm just a child!" I protested.

The amahs laughed. For some reason, they thought what I said was hilarious. They laughed so hard that they had to wipe their eyes with their handkerchiefs.

"What's so funny?" I asked.

"Bee, you're always saying that you're so grown up," Siew Cheh explained.

My cheeks felt hot. "I don't think that anymore," I said.

"Si geena," Yong Cheh said, but her voice was kind. "Your grandmother did not get a chance to see her grandchildren, but I must fulfill my promise to take care of all of you." She dabbed at her eyes with her handkerchief. "This is why I must go to the Japanese."

"Yong Cheh, if you promise to our mistress, how can you leave?" Eng Cheh said, her voice surprisingly firm. "Who will take care of Master when he come home? And who take care of Mam? Siew Cheh is good with children, they need her. I am useless. If I go to Japanese, at least, I do something good for family."

We were speechless because we had never heard Eng Cheh speak so much or so confidently before. She steadily met our gaze. "Please. Let me do my duty."

A few days later, Mr DeSouza came to the house to fetch Eng Cheh. She had packed all her belongings into a few cloth bundles. Her samfu and hair looked immaculate. Her face was pale, but she had a brave demeanour. She seemed completely different from the person who had whimpered at every mention of the Japanese.

Much had already been said and a river of tears shed in the past few days, so our final parting was brief. Mr DeSouza picked up Eng Cheh's belongings in spite of her protests. Yong Cheh,

Siew Cheh, and I took turns to say goodbye.

"Thank you so much for saving Papa," I said, feeling that no words could convey the gratitude I felt.

"Eat more hor, Miss," Eng Cheh replied. This was something she always said when I didn't finish my food. I didn't know why she was saying it now, but the familiar words struck a chord inside me.

I quietly watched Eng Cheh walk down the street with Mr DeSouza, heartbroken to lose another member of our little family.

NINETEEN

A noise woke me up in the middle of the night. I could hear people moving around downstairs. My heartbeat quickened. Had the looters returned? Or was it Japanese soldiers? I listened carefully. The stairs creaked, and footsteps approached my room. I shut my eyes tightly as I heard my door open. Someone was standing in the doorway, staring at me. My heart pounded in my chest, but I couldn't resist – I peeked.

In the orange glow of a candle, I saw my beloved Papa's face.

"Papa!" I ran so quickly at him that I almost knocked him off his feet.

Papa laughed. "I'm sorry I woke you, Bee. I just wanted to look at you."

The fear and worry that I had been keeping inside for the last few weeks suddenly overcame me.

"Shh, don't cry. You saved me, Bee!" Papa said.

"I thought I would never see you again," I said between sobs.

"I'm afraid that I made everyone worried. I'm terribly sorry."

"What happened, Papa?"

Just then, Siew Cheh came to tell Papa that his meal was ready. "Bee, you must be overjoyed to see your Pa, but why don't you let him eat and rest tonight? You can talk to him in the morning," she said.

Reluctantly, I went back to bed, but I was too excited to sleep. I had so many questions for Papa. Quietly, I crept downstairs and crouched in the dark corner under the stairs, where I could see and hear what was going on in the dining room.

Papa was seated at the table with an array of plates in front of him. Ma was next to him. Siew Cheh and Yong Cheh were sitting with them too. They were all listening to Papa.

"… banging on the front door. I thought the Japanese had come, just as Richard had telephoned to warn me that morning. He said they were targeting big houses, looking for valuables. That was why I wanted all of you to go into hiding."

Everyone nodded, eyes glued to Papa. He took another bite, then continued, "I opened the door, and can you believe it? It was a mob of local men, our own people!"

"Si lang kui!" Yong Cheh exclaimed.

"They rushed in and started snatching things. There was nothing I could do … then the Japanese military police arrived. I thought they were going to arrest the looters, but they fired into the air and let them run away. It turned out, the Kempeitei had come to arrest me."

Ma gasped. "Oh Henry! The Japanese arrested you?" She was the only one who hadn't known this.

Papa nodded gravely. "They suspected that I was a spy for the British."

"But that's terrible!" Ma exclaimed.

Papa patted her hand. "Calm down, dear. Can't you see I'm fine?" he said reassuringly. "They took me to their headquarters. For the first time in my life, I got to sit in the back of a lorry," Papa chuckled.

The amahs laughed, but Ma looked shocked. I shuddered as I thought of my nightmares where Papa was taken to the beach in a lorry.

Papa became serious again. "They kept me in a small room with seven other men. One of them was Mr Seet – you remember the manager at the Bank of China, dear?"

"Yes, nice man. He was there too?" Ma asked.

Papa nodded. "We didn't dare to speak in case the Kempeitai was secretly listening. Every few days, they would take someone out of the room. Sometimes, that man would be brought back, covered with bruises. Or we would not see him again, like Mr Seet. I don't know what happened to him."

"Poor man. I hope he's all right," Ma said, drying her eyes with her handkerchief.

Papa put his chopsticks down. "Twice, I was taken for interrogation. There was a Japanese officer who spoke English. He accused me of spying for the British. I told him I was just a businessman, but he didn't believe me. They forced me to the ground and stuck a rubber hose in my throat. Then they –"

"Ow!" I yelped from the sudden, sharp pain on my leg. Ying was really too much! Everyone turned in my direction.

"Bee Ling?" Ma called.

Sheepishly, I stepped out from my hiding place.

"Si geena," Yong Cheh scolded.

"Bee Ling, how long have you been there?" Papa asked.

"Sorry … I couldn't sleep."

To my relief, Papa smiled and said, "Since you're still awake, why don't you come and sit with us?"

Shamefaced but happy, I took the empty seat on Papa's other side. I felt self-conscious as he studied my face.

"You look well. You're a strong girl," he said approvingly.

I felt my cheeks flush, embarrassed that Papa was saying this in front of everyone.

He continued, "I'm so happy to see all of you. I was angry with myself for blocking your way out with the cupboard. How did you manage to come out?"

"Hmph!" Yong Cheh huffed and looked pointedly at me, making me wish I was still hiding under the stairs.

"Didn't you move the cupboard, Henry?" Ma asked.

"No, I didn't have a chance," Papa replied.

"Ask Bee Ling," Yong Cheh suggested gleefully.

Papa turned to me in surprise. "Bee? Sounds like you've been quite the heroine lately! What did you do?"

I gulped. What should I say? Should I tell him that Ying had saved us, that in fact, she has been back since the day of her funeral? Not to mention how she has been viciously pinching me again? Would Papa believe me? I knew that Ma would surely not and she would be angry with me.

"I uh … prayed hard, you know?" I said, looking at Ma for support. I could feel Yong Cheh boring a hole in my head with her glare.

"It was a miracle, Henry! A child's prayer is powerful," Ma said, beaming.

Yong Cheh snorted. Papa looked confused.

I quickly changed the subject. "Papa, how did Mr DeSouza get the Kempeitai to release you? He said there was a man called Shinso … suki?"

"Shinozaki. Mr Shinozaki is a high-ranking Japanese official, but he's different from the rest. Because of him, I'm still alive," Papa said.

"Why do you know this, Bee? And how is your teacher involved?" Ma asked.

"Bee phoned Mr DeSouza for help," Papa said. "Without them, I would not be here. But most of all, I owe my life to Eng Cheh."

"Eng Cheh?" Ma asked, confused. It was only then that she realised Eng Cheh was not with us.

We fell silent. Eng Cheh had seldom spoken, and it had been easy to forget that she was around, but at this moment, her absence was overwhelming.

TWENTY

It was nice to have Papa back home. He was different, but in a good way. He cleared away the hibiscus bush and bamboo in our back garden to grow vegetables. He spent the whole day outside – digging, planting and watering. His skin became deeply tanned, and instead of smart business clothes, he wore khaki shorts and white singlets. Ma joked that he looked like a trishaw rider.

At dinner, Papa would ask us what vegetables we wanted him to grow. He had already planted chilli, onion, yam and sweet potato. I suggested kangkong, and he agreed. Yong Cheh had a lot of advice for him because of her farming experience. She saved vegetable peels to make soil fertiliser, and she even suggested using Ming's poo, but Papa said it was unsanitary.

Sometimes, I would help Papa in the garden even though I was afraid of earthworms and centipedes. He taught me about plants and explained how they made food through a process called photosynthesis. It was like my Science lessons in school, but even better. Papa did not allow Yong Cheh to join him in the garden because he said that she talked too much and disturbed his peace. I think that made her jealous of me.

One afternoon, hot and sweaty from working in the garden,

I went to the kitchen for a drink. When she saw me, Yong Cheh remarked, "You are getting so dark from the sun, just like a kampong girl. Not like Ying, who had such beautiful, fair skin."

Yong Cheh had always enjoyed comparing me to Ying and pointing out that she was better than me. It used to drive me crazy, but this time, I simply said, "Of course, I'm not like Ying. I'm Bee Ling, remember?"

She stared at me with her mouth open and was speechless for once.

Our food was getting worse. Our porridge was increasingly watery, and we ate it with measly bits of pickled vegetables or salted fish. How I longed for a crispy chicken wing or the sweet and salty taste of pork floss. I even missed having a simple hardboiled egg. My empty stomach growled a lot, especially at night. At such times, I remembered with shame how I used to complain about my food.

There were many things that I had disliked eating, but I hated buah keluak the most. I remembered the last time that Yong Cheh had cooked it.

"Eee, they look like giant beetles," I said, wrinkling my nose at the ugly, black nuts.

"They do not," Ying said.

"Yes, they do," I insisted.

"I'll shell one for you," Papa said to me.

"Don't want! Yucks!" I cried.

"Just eat the shrimp and pork in the dish," Ma said.

"I don't want any part of it." I replied.

Papa shelled a buah keluak and put it on my plate. "Bee

Ling, I won't have this nonsense anymore," he said sternly. "You are not leaving this table until you eat it."

When Papa used that tone of voice, I didn't dare to argue. I quietly ate the rest of my food, but I did not touch the buah keluak.

We finished dinner, and Eng Cheh came to clear the dishes. When she reached for my plate, Papa said, "Leave it. She has to eat the buah keluak."

Eng Cheh nodded and cleared the rest of the table.

Yong Cheh brought in bubur cha cha, one of my favourite desserts. As she served it, Papa told her, "Don't give any to Bee Ling until she finishes her food."

Yong Cheh smirked as she took my bowl of bubur cha cha back to the kitchen.

I watched Ying eat the yam and sweet potatoes in cold coconut milk and stared at the disgusting lump on my plate. I sniffled and let my tears flow.

"Oh Henry," Ma said, "don't force the poor girl."

"She can't always get what she wants," Papa said firmly.

I started sobbing loudly, but Papa was not moved. Everyone finished dessert, and I was left alone with that horrid nut on my plate.

After some time, Ying came back. She had already bathed and changed into her pyjamas. "Look what Lucy gave us at her birthday party," she said, showing me a handful of sweets in colourful wrappers. "Her parents bought it from Robinsons. I'll give it to you if you finish that."

I wanted the sweets, but I knew that if I agreed, then everyone would praise Ying for getting me to eat buah keluak. She already had enough praise for the things that she did, why should she be praised for what I did too?

"No thanks," I said, sticking out my tongue at her.

"So childish! Please go to bed soon. I have to raise the flag at Assembly, so don't make me late again," Ying grumbled, and went upstairs.

Siew Cheh brought me a cup of barley with lemon. "I made it extra sweet. It will cover the taste," she said.

I drank the barley. It tasted good, but I still refused to eat the buah keluak. Siew Cheh sighed and went away.

After a while, Eng Cheh timidly came up to me. "Miss ah, quick eat so I can wash plate hor?"

"Just take it," I said.

"But Miss, your Papa –"

"Let's just say that I ate it," I whispered, and winked at her.

"Aiyoh cannot like that, Miss!" she said, looking scared.

Just then, Yong Cheh stomped up to the table. "Si geena! Finish your food so we can clean up! We are not waiting for you all night."

"Take it, take it," I said, holding the plate out to her.

"Do you know how much work went into that? I soaked it for five days!"

"Then why don't you eat it?"

"Si geena, this is your grandmother's recipe, the best in Singapore."

"Then you eat it!"

She glared at me fiercely, but I stared back at her, making sure not to blink. Finally, she snatched the plate from me and stomped to the kitchen, Eng Cheh following her.

"Don't forget my bubur cha cha," I called after them.

I felt guilty when I looked back on this. After what we had been eating the last few months, I would be thrilled to have buah kelauk. I couldn't wait for Papa's garden vegetables to grow. It would be nice to have sweet potatoes to add flavour to our porridge, and I couldn't wait to taste kangkong fried with chilli and onions again. We were lucky to have a mango tree. Every day, I checked on the green mangoes, impatient for them to ripen. The thought of sweet mangoes with sticky rice and coconut cream made my mouth water. Occasionally, Yong Cheh would make steamed buns with sugar and flour. It was such a treat that I would keep it in my pocket and take tiny bites throughout the day. It stopped my stomach from grumbling so much.

TWENTY-ONE

The Japanese Administration issued us with food ration cards. Papa said it was to control the food supply on the island. The yellow cards told us where to go and how much food we could buy. At first, Yong Cheh went to get the provisions, but she was in bad shape after just one trip. She had to walk a long way to the designated shop and then queue under the hot sun for hours. Afterwards, her feet were so sore that she had trouble walking for a week.

The following month, Papa decided to purchase the rations himself. Yong Cheh said that people with children were given priority in the queue, so I asked Papa if I could go with him.

"No," he said immediately.

"Please, Papa. I can walk fast, and I won't be tired at all."

"It's not safe."

"I'm not scared if I'm with you."

"Bee, it's not Singapore anymore. It's Syonan-to," Papa said.

"But you heard Yong Cheh, children get to go first," I persisted.

"Sir, the lines are very long. I went at six o'clock in the morning, but I still waited the whole day," Yong Cheh said.

"I will wait for as long as it takes," Papa answered, annoyed.

"Sir, what if we dressed Bee up as a boy?" Siew Cheh suggested.

"Not you too?" Papa looked at Siew Cheh in surprise.

Siew Cheh blushed. "Sorry, sir. Little girls are dressing up as boys to be safe."

"Yes, I want to be a boy!" I exclaimed excitedly. "It will be a great adventure. Please, Papa! I haven't gone out for so long."

"Ah, so the truth is that you want an adventure, and not that you want to help," Papa said, smiling.

"But I do want to help you," I insisted.

Papa sighed. "Let's see how you look as a boy."

"Yay!" I squealed. I was so excited that I hugged Papa, Siew Cheh, and even Yong Cheh.

"Gila!" Yong Cheh scolded, but she laughed.

A few days later, I was dressed and ready for my trip with Papa at five o'clock in the morning. Siew Cheh had altered a pair of Papa's old trousers so that it would fit me. I wore it with the white shirt from my school uniform. Siew Cheh pinned my hair up at the back, and I donned one of Papa's flat caps. I thought I looked quite handsome as a boy.

The sun had not yet come up, and the weather was cool. Papa said that we should walk quickly and not talk. We strode briskly through the dark, empty streets, our footsteps sounding strangely loud to my ears. Soon we passed our church, and further along, St Mary's Primary School. There was a big padlock on the gate, and the windows were dark, but the buildings looked the same. From the outside, you could not tell that it had been bombed. Still, something had changed, and it did not feel like the place which held so many happy memories for me. Papa squeezed my shoulder and gently led me away.

Whenever we passed someone, I noticed that they were

walking with their head down. This made me nervous, but soon, we heard birds chirping, and the sky started to lighten. Ahead of us, I could see the sun rising from the sea – a giant ball of red light.

"Papa, look!" I said excitedly.

Papa smiled but put a finger to his lips, reminding me not to talk. I thought of the mornings he had driven Ying and me to school. I was always sleepy and grumpy, while Ying was irritatingly chirpy. She always asked me to look at the sunrise, but I ignored her and kept my eyes closed, trying to catch more sleep. I wished she was here, so that I could tell her that she was right – it was magical.

The day turned hot and bright. My legs were aching, but I did not slow down. We saw some Japanese soldiers along the way. Each time, even if they were on the other side of the road, Papa and I would stop and bow until they had passed. I had already practiced bowing at home. Yong Cheh said it was important to bow low or the soldiers would beat you. We continued walking, and I knew we were getting close when more and more people were going the same way.

The shop was a big wooden shack in the middle of a dusty compound. Under the tin roof, there were barrels of rice, flour, sugar and other produce. I counted four shopkeepers, each serving a long line of customers. Although there were many people, things were orderly. Everyone queued up quietly, holding the yellow ration cards. I noticed a Japanese soldier in the shade of a large angsana tree, a rifle slung on his shoulder.

Papa and I joined one of the queues, but a kind Indian lady pointed us to a shorter line reserved for those with children. The sun rose until it was directly above us. It beat down so fiercely that I was sure smoke would rise from the top of my head. When it was almost our turn, a commotion broke out. The woman in front of us was arguing with the shopkeeper in a Chinese dialect. The woman shouted and pointed at the weighing scale, and the shopkeeper yelled back at her. I found it was quite exciting, but Papa pulled me back.

As the quarrel got more heated, the woman slapped the shopkeeper and he pushed her to the ground. Some people rushed forward to get between them, jostling Papa and me. Suddenly, a gunshot rang out! I screamed, and Papa immediately shielded me with his body. From under Papa's arm, I saw the Japanese soldier approaching.

My heart beat loudly as the soldier stopped in front of the woman. He was standing so close to us that I could see the beads of perspiration above his lips. He extended a hand to the woman on the ground and pulled her to her feet. I did not expect what happened next – the soldier slapped the woman. I flinched as the sharp sound cut through the air. The woman yelped and stumbled backward. Then the soldier turned to the shopkeeper and, with a quick jab of his arm, knocked him in the head with the butt of his rifle. The shopkeeper grunted and sank to his knees, clutching his head. No one moved or made a sound as the soldier walked back to his spot under the tree.

The woman quietly picked up her bags and left. The shopkeeper got to his feet and motioned for Papa to come forward. As he weighed our provisions and stamped our ration card, I couldn't help staring at the large purple bruise growing on the side of his head. It reminded me of a dragonfruit.

As much as I had looked forward to our trip, I couldn't wait to get home. Papa was right – it was no longer Singapore, it was Syonan-to.

TWENTY-TWO

We were getting used to life under the Japanese Occupation. We didn't hear gunshots as often, and we finally had sweet potatoes to put in our porridge. My stomach was growling less at night. Ming was growing quickly. He was eating porridge and had started crawling. I had to watch him carefully because he could be quite fast.

We almost had a mishap one time. I was so engrossed in my book that I didn't realise that Ming had crawled out of my room. When I finally went to look for him, I saw him perched at the top of the stairs.

"Ming!" I screamed.

He did not respond. His eyes were focused on something in front of him, and he was smiling. I ran over to pick Ming up, and a wave of cold air went through me. My spine tingled, and I knew that Ying had been watching him. I was sure that she had kept him from falling down the stairs. I promised myself that I would take better care of Ming.

A wonderful development was that Mr DeSouza had started tutoring Janet and me again. Three times a week, he fetched Janet to my house on his bicycle. Just like when I had gone with Papa to buy provisions, Janet dressed as a boy during these trips. She didn't have to wear a hat because her mother had cut her hair short. She cried about it for a week, but she cheered up once she started riding with Mr DeSouza. Annoyingly, she wouldn't stop talking about it.

"It's so romantic. Just the two of us," she said.

"Just the two of you? On the road?" I scoffed.

"I mean that it's just the two of us on the bicycle."

"Oh, really? I thought it was a circus bicycle with five clowns and ten baboons," I answered crossly.

"Don't be jealous, Bee! I wish you could be there too."

"I guess I'm a bit jealous," I admitted.

"Well, of course, you should be! Do you know how good he smells?"

"Really? What does he smell like?"

"Mmm… soap!"

"What kind of soap?"

"I think, Lux soap."

"I use Lux soap too!" I said happily.

"Me too!" Janet laughed.

I enjoyed our lessons. I especially loved reading books and talking about them with Mr DeSouza. One of my favourites was *Pride and Prejudice* by Jane Austen. Janet and I thought that it was romantic, and we enjoyed discussing the topic of marriage with Mr DeSouza.

"How does Mrs. Bennett choose husbands for her daughters?" he asked.

"By their wealth," I answered.

"Good. What do you think of this practice?" he asked.

"I think handsome-ness is more important," Janet answered.

Mr DeSouza smiled. "So would you marry George Wickham?"

"No, of course not!" Janet huffed.

"But he's handsome," Mr DeSouza said, a glint in his eye.

"He's also dishonest and evil," I pointed out.

"Yah, no thanks!" Janet said.

"So what qualities do you think are important in a future husband?" Mr DeSouza asked.

"Honesty, bravery, kindness …" I answered.

"And handsome-ness," Janet insisted.

"Sure. It's important to like, if not love, the person you're going to marry," Mr DeSouza said. "Unfortunately, not everyone gets to choose whom they marry."

"Ma's relatives tried to arrange a marriage for her. Luckily, she ran away," I said.

"That's very fortunate. Thanks for sharing, Bee Ling," Mr DeSouza said.

Encouraged by his response, I added, "And Siew Cheh was almost sold as a mui tsai – you know, a slave girl – but Papa took her in."

I was pleased when this made Mr DeSouza stare at me for a full minute, too shocked to say anything.

Janet never missed a good opportunity, so she asked, "What qualities do you want in your future wife, Mr Dee?"

To our great delight, Mr DeSouza forgot his rule about personal questions. "Well, someone I can get along with, someone who makes me laugh –"

This made us giggle, which was too bad because Mr DeSouza turned pink and changed the subject. When Siew Cheh brought us drinks later, I noticed Mr DeSouza staring at her even more than usual.

Papa had a surprise for me. I followed him to the back garden excitedly.

"See that over there?" Papa asked, pointing to a rectangular shape under a sack cloth. "It's for you."

I ran over and immediately heard chickens! I didn't want to disappoint Papa, so when I lifted the cloth and saw a wire coop with three chickens inside, I acted surprised.

"Oh wow! Chickens! Are they my very own?"

"Yes, Bee. You've been doing such a good job taking care of Ming, I think you deserve it."

Impatiently, I unlatched the little door and let the chickens out. There was a fat one with white feathers, a small brown one, and one with black and white spots. I immediately loved all of them.

"I'm going to name them Fatty, Brownie and Spotty!"

Papa laughed. "Good job! I can already tell who's who."

Every morning, even before I brushed my teeth, I would run downstairs to feed my new pets. I scattered grain on the ground and watched them peck in a frenzy. Every evening, I made sure that they were safely inside the coop before I latched the little wire door. Then I put the sack cloth over the cage. I was afraid that an owl or a cat would get them.

One of my favourite things to do was taking Ming to see the chickens. I let him crawl on the ground among them even though Siew Cheh complained that it made him dirty. One day, I pointed to the chickens, saying "puck puck" and was surprised when Ming echoed me.

"Puk puk," Ming said, looking at Brownie.

"That's right, Ming! Puck puck," I laughed.

"Puk puk, puk puk," Ming repeated as he crawled towards Fatty. He reached for her, but she flew off, and Ming burst out crying.

"Aww, don't cry. She likes you, she just doesn't want you to catch her," I told him.

But Ming was determined. He went after Spotty next, and when he couldn't get her, he turned his attention to Brownie. It was a game of catch, with Ming chasing the chickens and chanting "puk puk".

I laughed so much that it brought Papa and the amahs out of the house. Papa was delighted and said that Ma should see this, so he fetched her. Soon, we were all laughing and clucking like chickens.

A cool breeze ruffled my hair, carrying with it the sweet scent of frangipani. I turned to the frangipani tree and saw Ying, a lone figure under the flowering branches. She was watching us.

TWENTY-THREE

It was about nine months into the Japanese Occupation, and Ming's first birthday was approaching. Papa announced that we would have a small birthday celebration with close friends. I asked if we could invite Janet and Mr DeSouza, and Papa agreed.

Fortuitously, my chickens had started laying eggs. I had gone out to feed them as usual when I almost stepped on an egg in the grass. I picked it up carefully and went to show Papa. He congratulated me, and I felt like a proud mother hen.

Over the next few days, I found more and more eggs. Yong Cheh suggested all sorts of ways to cook them – frying with salty chye por, braising in dark soya sauce, or steaming until it was light and airy. All her suggestions were tempting, but I wanted to save them to make red eggs for Ming's birthday.

"That's a wonderful idea, but since they're your eggs, you should have one now," Papa said.

"No thanks, I'll wait," I told him. For some reason, saving the eggs for Ming made me happy. Papa smiled, and I knew that he approved.

Ma was busy with preparations for Ming's birthday. She wanted to make new clothes for him, but all her beautiful fabrics had been stolen. A strange thing that we had discovered was that the looters had not taken Ying's clothes. They had ransacked her room and stolen everything else, but they did not touch her beautiful dresses. Yong Cheh explained that many people knew that Ying had died in the bombing, and no one dared to take her clothes for fear that it would bring them bad luck.

I was having lunch with Ma and Papa when Siew Cheh reminded Ma of this. "Mam, for Ming's birthday outfit, we can use one of Ying's dresses for the material."

Ma lowered her head, but not before I saw the tears in her eyes.

Siew Cheh noticed it too. "I'm sorry, Mam! I didn't mean to upset you. I –"

"It's all right, Siew Cheh. You did nothing wrong. You can go now," Papa said gently. When Siew Cheh left, Papa reached across the table and put his hand over Ma's. "You know, dear, Ying will always be in our memories, but she doesn't need her clothes anymore."

Ma made an anguished sound. Her chair scraped the floor loudly as she left the table. Papa immediately went after her, leaving me alone with my watery porridge. I wondered if Ma would ever get over Ying.

"Why don't you go and comfort Ma?" I said aloud to the empty room, but there was no reply. At such times, I wondered why Ying only appeared to me and not Ma or anyone else.

Yong Cheh was stockpiling food for the birthday celebration by doing what she could to scrimp and save from our daily meals.

Thankfully, Papa's work on the vegetable garden was paying off. Yong Cheh said that she was excited to cook a "real meal" again.

One evening, during dinner, Yong Cheh said, "Sir, I think for Ming's birthday, we should have roast chicken."

I gasped. "You're not thinking about my chickens, are you?"

Yong Cheh acted like she couldn't hear me and continued addressing Papa. "It's a special occasion, marking the first year for the young master of the family. Usually, I would suggest a roast pig, but under these circumstances, we should have two, maybe three, roast chickens."

"No way!" I yelled, jumping up so fast that my chair crashed to the ground.

"Behave yourself, Bee Ling," Papa said, giving me a stern look.

I picked up the chair and sat down. "Please, Papa. I love Fatty, Brownie and Spotty," I begged.

Yong Cheh burst out laughing, "Aiyoh! You named the chickens ah?"

"Of course. They're my pets," I answered, glaring at her.

"Chickens are not pets! Who gives names to chickens? Si geena!" She laughed so hard that tears were rolling down her face.

My own tears were also falling because I could see that Papa was considering her evil suggestion. He turned to Ma, "Bee has been taking good care of the chickens, but Yong Cheh has a point. What do you think, dear?"

Ma did not look at me. "Henry, did you give the chickens to Bee?" she asked.

"Yes, I did," Papa replied.

"Then they are Bee's chickens, and she should decide," Ma said.

"Thank you, Ma!" I exclaimed, running over to give her a big hug.

"Bee, you're going to bruise me," she said, smiling.

I let her go and gave Yong Cheh the biggest smirk I could muster.

Unfortunately, Yong Cheh did not give up. Over the next few days, she kept hounding me. The final straw came when she crept up on me while I was feeding the chickens one morning.

"Maybe that fat, white one will be enough."

I didn't know she was there, and I jumped. "Yong Cheh, you better stay away from my chickens! They're mine."

"Does that mean you should keep them all to yourself?" she asked.

"Yes! Don't you dare steal them! I know you're a thief. I saw you stealing Ma's jewellery from right there" I said, pointing to the mango tree. "If you touch my chickens, I will tell Papa what you did!"

Yong Cheh stared at me for a long moment, looking shocked. Then she clucked her tongue in an irritating way and shook her head. "Si geena, where did you even come from? You're so different from Ying," she said musingly.

"So? Why do you always compare me to Ying?" I asked.

"Do you know that Ying looks so much like your grandmother? Madam Neo was the kindest, most beautiful lady I have ever met in my life. Ying was just like her, but you! You're not like her granddaughter at all."

I had never heard this before, and Yong Cheh's words stung. "You're a mean, horrible orang utan!" I yelled.

Yong Cheh clucked her tongue again. "You see? You see? Ying would never talk like this. She was – Ow!" Yong Cheh suddenly squawked and clutched her arm.

I laughed, happy to know that Ying was on my side. "I think you got pinched for saying the wrong thing," I sniggered.

Sure enough, we could see a blue-black mark forming on Yong Cheh's fleshy arm. Looking around fearfully, she whispered, "Si geena, you better listen! Don't just think about yourself. If you love your little brother, let him have a chicken." She rubbed the bruise on her arm and added, "And if you care about your sister, let her go." With that, she turned and hurried back to the house.

I tried to ignore Yong Cheh, but I wondered what she meant. I sat under the frangipani tree, breathing in the sweet scent of its flowers. Tears came to my eyes as I thought of Ying, my annoying, bossy sister.

"Ying, do you want to leave? Where will you go?" I asked aloud. "And what will I do without you?"

But I only heard the chickens clucking as the sun continued to rise in the sky.

TWENTY-FOUR

The day finally arrived. Ming's birthday celebration was starting at noon. Ma and Siew Cheh had made him a cute outfit from Papa's old shirts. They even made a little red bow tie.

Since I didn't have a nice dress, Janet offered to lend me one. She showed up at ten o'clock in the morning with one of her amahs carrying a big dress box. We went up to my room, and her amah went to help in the kitchen. Janet placed the box on my bed and pulled out a beautiful blue dress.

"That's for me?"

"I told you I would bring you something nice, right? I haven't even worn it yet," she said proudly as she handed it to me.

"Thank you, Janet." I was touched.

"Well, what are you waiting for? Put it on!"

"Can you leave the room?"

Janet giggled and went out. I slipped on the dress and zipped it up. The material was light and soft, and it fit me nicely.

Janet came back and scrutinised me. "Turn around," she instructed.

I made a slow spin, feeling self-conscious.

"You know what you need?" she asked.

"What?"

"A bra," she said matter-of-factly.

"What? No way!"

"Go look in the mirror."

"I already looked!"

"Well, you need *something*, at least a singlet," she insisted.

I walked over to the mirror and was mortified to see what Janet meant. I immediately crossed my arms over my chest.

"I ... I don't have anything," I said, my cheeks burning.

"I could have brought you one of mine, but it's too late now," she said.

"I can't wear this then," I said, disappointed.

"Wait, can't you borrow one of Ying's?"

"I don't think Ma would like that."

"Why?"

"Just trust me on this," I told her.

"Look, everyone is so busy right now. Who's going to notice?" Janet persisted.

Ying had never liked me borrowing her things, and it was possible that *she* would notice, but I couldn't tell Janet that.

"Come on!" Janet said, grabbing my hand and dragging me out of the room. "Stop acting like that, okay? Everyone has neh-neh!"

We went across the hall and slipped into Ying's room. It was clean and tidy as ever. The shelves were lined with books, and the bed was neatly covered with a pink bedspread. Janet carefully closed the door behind us and tiptoed to the cupboard. I hung back nervously, waiting for Ying to pinch me or do something worse.

Janet opened the cupboard. "Wah! Look at all these," she whispered, riffling through Ying's dresses.

I was annoyed to see her touching Ying's things. "We don't

have time for this," I said, pushing her out of the way. "Let me get it."

When Janet stepped back, a bottom drawer slid open, revealing white singlets folded neatly inside. I picked up the top one and closed the drawer, glad that I had Ying's permission.

Janet and I spent the next hour curling each other's hair, then excitedly, we bounded downstairs. Yong Cheh had really outdone herself. There was a wonderful spread on the dining table, and right in the centre were my eggs! I was thrilled that I had managed to save twenty-eight of them. The eggs were dyed bright red and arranged in a pyramid. With a pang, I remembered that I had wanted to help make them.

"Why didn't you let me dye the eggs?" I complained when Siew Cheh walked in.

"You were busy getting ready."

"But I told you that I wanted to. They are my eggs, you know!"

"Si geena! You better take your nonsense elsewhere. We have no time for this," Yong Cheh scolded.

Janet's eyes widened with surprise. When we were out of earshot, she asked, "How can your amah talk to you like that?"

"Yong Cheh is always like that," I told her.

"I wouldn't stand for it," she said haughtily.

Papa stood in the living room to welcome the guests. He had not seen them since the Japanese Occupation began. There were smiles and tears as Papa greeted his old friends.

Janet and I eagerly waited for Mr DeSouza to arrive. We were excited even though we had seen him for class just three days ago. When he walked in, wearing a smart white shirt, we looked at each other and giggled. As promised, he brought a record player. He set it up in a corner of the room and let us select the records. It was lovely to hear music playing in the house again.

Siew Cheh served everyone drinks, then Ma came downstairs with Ming. She looked beautiful even though she was dressed in a plain cotton cheongsam. Ming looked adorable in his new clothes. I could tell that he loved the attention because he was smiling and babbling at everyone. Papa gave a little speech to thank the guests for coming, then we started eating.

Janet and I filled our plates and settled in the corner under the stairs. This was the perfect spot to spy on Mr DeSouza. He was playing peekaboo with Ming who was in Siew Cheh's arms.

"Isn't he going to eat?" Janet asked.

It appeared that Siew Cheh was asking Mr DeSouza the same question because she was gesturing towards the food. We could not hear what he said, but they both laughed.

"Remember what he said? He wants a girlfriend who makes him laugh," I said.

As if on cue, Mr DeSouza laughed again.

"Wait, are you saying that he likes your servant?" Janet asked, surprised.

"Haven't you noticed the way he acts when she brings the drinks?"

"What do you mean?"

"He always looks so shy," I said, "and he thanks her so politely."

"That's because he's a shy and polite person," Janet replied.

"Hmph," I muttered, not wanting to argue.

We ate our food, which tasted delicious, and continued watching Mr DeSouza. Siew Cheh passed Ming to him and went to the dining table. He made funny faces which did not amuse Ming but sent Janet and me into fits of giggles. Siew

Cheh came back with a plate of food and handed it to Mr DeSouza. Then she took Ming and walked away. Unaware that we were observing him, Mr DeSouza followed Siew Cheh with his eyes as she crossed the room. It was obvious, even to Janet, that he had a crush on Siew Cheh.

"I can't believe it," she fumed.

"Why? Siew Cheh is very pretty, don't you think? And she's nice too."

"But she's a servant," Janet said. "She's not good enough for him."

I disagreed with Janet, but I didn't say anything. I had always loved Siew Cheh and thought of her as my own family. The only thing that had disappointed me was when I saw her stealing Ma's jewellery with the other amahs. I would soon come to regret it, but in that moment, I decided to tell Janet.

She was outraged. "Are you sure your amahs stole from your family?"

"I saw it with my own eyes."

"Oh my God, Bee! Why haven't you told your parents?"

"Because Ma got sick and everything …" I tried to explain.

"Listen, this is like *Pride and Prejudice*, okay? Siew Cheh is George Wickham, a dishonest person pretending to be someone else. We can't let Mr Dee fall into her trap!"

"Trap?"

"Didn't you see her stealing from your family? That means she's a thief, right?"

I nodded weakly.

"We have to save Mr Dee!" Janet declared, her eyes flashing.

"We do?"

"Don't worry, I'll think of a plan," she said. "Just leave it to me."

Suddenly, I had a stomachache and couldn't eat anymore. Just then, we heard Mr DeSouza calling us. "Bee Ling? Janet? It's time to change the record."

When lunch was over, Yong Cheh brought out a big birthday cake. Ma sat in front of the cake with Ming, and everyone gathered around to sing the birthday song. To our delight, Ming blew out the candle himself. We clapped and cheered.

A draught of cold air made the back of my neck tingle. I turned and saw Ying standing in a far corner of the room, watching us. I couldn't be sure, but I thought that she looked sad. It occurred to me that Ying used to be the centre of attention, but now she was always apart from everyone. I wondered if she was lonely.

That night, I placed a red egg that I had secretly squirrelled away for her on my windowsill, next to the bookmark and hairpin.

"Ying, this red egg is for you. Please enjoy it before the ants come," I said.

Suddenly, I felt as if the weight of the world was on my shoulders. I was worried about Ying, I was upset that my chest was growing, and worst of all, I dreaded what Janet was planning to do about Siew Cheh and Mr DeSouza.

TWENTY-FIVE

I had a sick feeling in my stomach when I woke up. We were having class later, and I was afraid of what would happen. I wondered if Janet would tell Mr DeSouza about Siew Cheh on their way here, but all seemed normal when they arrived.

Our lesson proceeded as usual in the first hour. We were working on Maths questions when Siew Cheh came in with drinks. Mr DeSouza's face lit up when he saw her.

"How are you, Siew Cheh?" he asked.

"I'm well, sir. Thank you for asking," she answered shyly.

Mr DeSouza laughed. "I'm Phillip, remember? Who is this 'sir' you keep mentioning?"

Siew Cheh blushed.

Mr DeSouza held up his cup as if he was making a toast. "Siew Cheh, you make the best barley drink!" he declared and took a huge gulp.

"No, no," Siew Cheh protested, "there's not enough barley or sugar."

"I think it's perfect the way it is!" he said, making her blush even more.

From across the table, Janet rolled her eyes. The knot in my stomach tightened.

When Siew Cheh left the room, Janet immediately launched into action. "Mr Dee, remember *Pride and Prejudice*?" she asked.

"Yes, why?" Mr DeSouza asked, confused.

"Remember you asked if I would marry George Wickham because he's handsome?"

"Yes?"

"And I said no because he's dishonest, right, Bee?" Janet asked, turning to me.

I nodded weakly, wishing that she would leave me out of this.

She calmly continued, "I think all of us agree that we shouldn't marry a dishonest person, right, Mr Dee?"

"That's true," Mr DeSouza said, looking puzzled.

"So Bee and I think that you need to know something. It's about Siew Cheh."

"What do you mean?" Mr DeSouza asked, turning to me. His face had suddenly turned pink.

"Tell him, Bee," Janet said.

Mr DeSouza waited expectantly. My face felt hot, and I wished that I could disappear on the spot. But as if I was in a bad dream, I found myself telling him that during Ying's funeral, I had seen the amahs, including Siew Cheh, digging in the back garden and stealing Ma's jewellery.

I would never forget the look on Mr DeSouza's face. His eyes clouded, and he seemed lost. He was silent for a long moment.

"Excuse me," he finally said, and left the room.

Across the table, Janet grinned triumphantly. "Good job, Bee!" she crowed.

I wanted to throw something at her head, but instead, I choked back a sob and ran to my room.

Things changed after that. Mr DeSouza was no longer his usual cheerful self. He went through our lessons in a brisk, methodical way. When Siew Cheh brought us drinks, he thanked her politely, but he didn't try to joke or make conversation with her. I also noticed that he didn't drink any more barley.

I wondered what Siew Cheh thought of the abrupt change in Mr DeSouza. I imagined that she was heartbroken, but I did not dare to ask. I avoided her as much as I could because I knew that I had done something terrible.

TWENTY-SIX

One night, a big thunderstorm rattled the house. Rain lashed the windows and tree branches slapped against the roof. The noises from the storm caused me to drift in and out of sleep. At some point, I heard Ying calling my name. I got out of bed and went to her room. She was waiting for me in her bed.

"Here," she said, lifting her blanket and making space for me.

I climbed in and lay next to her. She pulled the blanket over us. "Don't be scared," Ying said.

As sleep came over me, I heard Ming crying. The storm was loud, but Ming's faint cry was unmistakable.

"Wake up, Bee!" Ying said urgently, shaking me.

I opened my eyes and found myself in my own bed. Ying was nowhere in sight, but I could still hear Ming crying. There was something different about his cry, and it frightened me. I ran to Ming's room and picked him up. His little body was burning, and his clothes were wet with sweat. I carried him to Ma and Papa's room.

Our telephone did not work anymore, so Papa put on a raincoat and went out into the storm to look for Dr Oei. I fell asleep before he returned with the doctor.

The next day, I learned the terrible news that Ming had malaria. It was a serious illness spread by mosquitos. According to Dr Oei's instructions, mosquito nets were set up around Ming's cot. He said that the medicine for malaria, called quinine, was no longer available because of the war. We could only keep Ming comfortable and hope for the best.

Ma, Siew Cheh and I took turns taking care of Ming. It was obvious that he was in pain. He cried a lot. I tried to keep him cool by placing wet washcloths on his forehead and giving him water to drink. When he vomited, I cleaned him and changed his clothes. Ming liked it when I carried him around the room and sang to him. I sang everything I could think of, from nursery rhymes, such as *Mary Had a Little Lamb*, to Sunday School songs, like *Jesus Loves Me*, and popular American songs, including *Somewhere Over The Rainbow*. I knew that Ming enjoyed my singing because he made cooing sounds along with me. My arms, legs and back began to ache from carrying Ming so much.

Thankfully, on the fifth day, Ming's fever broke. I was delighted when he finished the bowl of porridge that I fed him. When I brought the empty bowl to the kitchen, Yong Cheh was at the sink doing the dishes. She said that since Ming's appetite had returned, we should give him something more nutritious to ensure a full recovery. Without looking at me, she added that the best thing for Ming would be chicken soup.

I felt a pang as I wondered who I would have to lose – Spotty, Brownie or Fatty.

"Okay," I said, "you can take one of my chickens."

Yong Cheh turned to me in surprise. "Wah, what a good big sister you are!" She smiled approvingly.

I quickly walked away before the tears came.

Later, as I was helping Siew Cheh with Ming's bath, he grabbed my hair and said, "chi chi". My heart skipped with joy to hear Ming calling me his big sister.

Excitedly, I ran to tell Ma. She smiled and said it was what I used to call Ying when I was younger. She continued, "Ying used to take care of you the way you're taking care of Ming now."

"She did?" I asked, wondering why we were talking about Ying.

"Yes, she really doted on you. She was such a good big sister," Ma said with a wistful smile.

Something exploded inside me. I had worked so hard to take care of Ming, but Ma did not say that I was a "good big sister". Instead, she was still singing Ying's praises.

"You really think that Ying was so great?" I demanded, tears springing to my eyes. Ma was shocked at my tone of voice, but I didn't care.

"You always praised her! There were times when she was mean to me, and she pinched me a lot, but you always took her side. And now, even when she's dead, you only think of her! You never notice the things that I do. You don't even care about me or Ming –"

"Stop it!" I heard Ma say as I felt her stinging slap.

Before I could react, a sharp sound startled us. The large oval mirror on Ma's dressing table had cracked from top to bottom!

Ma gaped at the mirror, her face as white as a sheet. "Ying!" she gasped.

And then I saw. Ying was reflected in a corner of the broken mirror. I turned to the other side of the room, but she was not there. When I looked back at the mirror, she was gone.

Ma crossed herself and dropped to her knees to pray.

Feeling hot and dizzy, I ran out of the room, down the stairs and through the kitchen, heading for the garden. When I stepped outside, the sunlight dazzled me. I continued forward blindly, but I felt my knees buckle. Then everything turned dark.

TWENTY-SEVEN

Dr Oei said it was what he had been afraid of. Malaria had spread in our home. Not only did I have it, but Yong Cheh had also contracted it. For the next few days, I lay in bed with high fever and chills. Everything hurt, including my eyes. I couldn't eat. Even water made me throw up.

Ma and Siew Cheh took turns taking care of me. I was surprised when one evening, Ma brought in a basin of water to give me a bath.

"Where's Siew Cheh?" I asked.

"She's looking after Yong Cheh. You want her?"

"No."

"I can take care of you too, you know," Ma said, smiling.

"Thank you, Ma."

"No need to thank me, silly."

I closed my eyes and enjoyed the feel of the cool washcloth against my feverish skin.

For the next few days, Ma fed and bathed me. One night, my fever soared, and my body shook with chills. Ma stayed by my side, a worried look on her face.

"Is there anything I can do to make you feel better?" she asked.

I remembered how much Ming had enjoyed my singing, so I asked Ma if she could sing to me.

In her soft, pretty voice, Ma sang the hymn, *What A Friend We Have In Jesus*. I closed my eyes, and the song soothed me to sleep.

The next morning, I woke up and found that my body felt cool and relaxed. I knew that I was better. Ma and Papa were pleased when I said I was hungry. Siew Cheh brought me some porridge with sweet potatoes. "Bee, I'm so happy you're getting well," she said.

"What about Yong Cheh?" I asked.

"She's still weak," Siew Cheh said sadly.

I suddenly remembered something. "Did Yong Cheh make the chicken soup for Ming?"

"Oh I have a funny story about that!"

"What? What happened?" I asked impatiently.

"Well, Yong Cheh was in the back garden, a chopping knife in one hand and a chicken in the other –"

"Which chicken?"

"Just listen, Bee. She was about to cut off the chicken's head –"

"What!"

"Oh sorry, I shouldn't have said that. But then, she had a dizzy spell and fainted. When I went outside and saw Yong Cheh lying there, with the chopper and the chicken next to her, I panicked! I ran into the house and told your Pa, 'Sir, I think the chicken has killed Yong Cheh!'"

"No way!" I burst out laughing.

"I don't know what I was thinking," Siew Cheh chuckled.

I was glad when she assured me that all my chickens were unharmed, but with a stab of guilt, I remembered what Janet and I had done.

When Ma and Papa were convinced that I had made a full recovery, I was allowed to go outside. I was glad to see my pet chickens again.

Yong Cheh, however, was getting weaker. She could not go to a hospital because they were now reserved for the Japanese military. I had always considered Yong Cheh as my enemy for scolding, criticising and telling on me, but I was worried about her. She was annoying, but I now saw that she was a part of my family. So I made up my mind. I told Papa that in order to help Yong Cheh get well, I would like her to have some chicken soup.

"Are you sure?" he asked, surprised.

I nodded, trying my best not to cry.

"How kind of you! I'm sure Yong Cheh will appreciate it," he said.

The next morning, I heard Papa telling Siew Cheh to prepare chicken soup, so I decided to stay in my room for the rest of the day.

In the afternoon, there was a soft knock on my door. It was Siew Cheh. I was reading a book in bed, and she came over and sat on the floor next to me. She looked guilty, so I knew that the chicken soup had been made.

"Bee ah, the soup is ready."

"Ugh, why must you tell me?"

"You've done a kind thing for Yong Cheh. Your Pa says that you should bring it to her yourself."

"No, I don't want to touch it."

"Yong Cheh will want to thank you."

"It's okay."

"Please, Bee?"

I glared at her. "Were you the one who killed my chicken?"

"It was my job, but I couldn't do it. I just couldn't," she said apologetically.

"Then who?"

"Your Pa."

"Papa?" I asked, surprised.

"It was hard for him too … That's why you shouldn't name chickens," Siew Cheh said. I realised that I wasn't the only one who felt bad about this.

"Who was it?" I asked.

Siew Cheh didn't reply.

"Was it Spotty?"

She shook her head.

"Brownie?"

She shook her head again.

"Oh poor Fatty!" I cried, burying my head under the pillow.

Siew Cheh patted my shoulder and left the room. Once I finished crying, I said a little prayer for Fatty and went downstairs.

TWENTY-EIGHT

I had not seen Yong Cheh since she had taken ill, and I was shocked at how different she looked. She was propped up against some pillows, her eyes closed. Siew Cheh was feeding her soup.

"Bee is here," Siew Cheh announced with a smile.

Yong Cheh's eyes fluttered open. She had lost so much weight that her cheeks were hollow, but what frightened me the most were her deep, dark eye sockets. I gave her a little wave, and she nodded weakly. We didn't say anything. I stood at the foot of the bed watching her take small sips of soup. After a while, she put up her hand to say she had enough. Siew Cheh wiped her lips with a handkerchief and left the room.

Yong Cheh beckoned to me. Nervously, I moved closer. I told myself it was only Yong Cheh, but her face had a greyish hue and her sunken eyes looked strange.

"Thank you, Miss," Yong Cheh said, her voice barely a whisper.

Tears filled my eyes. It was the first time she had ever called me "Miss". I gave a silly laugh. "I'm Bee, remember? Who are you calling 'Miss'?"

She smiled. "Don't cry," she said. "I'm going to see my

family. And dear Madam Neo. I will tell her she has a good granddaughter."

Yong Cheh passed away the next day. A large tent was set up in the back garden for the wake. Many amahs came to pay their respects, their uniforms turning the place into a sea of black and white.

We were glad when Eng Cheh showed up. We had not seen her since she had left, and it was good to know that she was doing well. Papa brought her to his study so that he could thank her for saving his life.

The wake continued late into the night. Although many tears were shed for Yong Cheh, the general atmosphere was like a party, with people talking, laughing, eating and playing mahjong. I stayed by Papa's side, enjoying the stories of Yong Cheh that were being told. I learned a lot of things about her, like how she was afraid of dogs. An elderly amah told a story of how Yong Cheh had once jumped into a longkang to avoid a pack of stray dogs. Unfortunately for her, the night-soil man had emptied his buckets into the drain, and she found herself knee-deep in human waste. She screamed so loudly that she frightened all the dogs away. Everyone laughed and agreed that Yong Cheh had a powerful voice.

Then Papa shared a story about Yong Cheh's loyal service to our family. He said that just before the Japanese invasion, he had buried Ma's wedding jewellery in the garden. I was sleepy at the time, but I immediately perked up.

According to Papa, Yong Cheh had learned that many people were burying their valuables in the garden, and thieves were aware of it. She advised Papa to let her keep Ma's jewellery safe. He trusted her, so he asked her to do what she thought best.

My mind replayed the scene that I had witnessed – the amahs under the mango tree, holding bags of Ma's jewellery. What had I really seen?

Papa continued to say that after the invasion, the Japanese had demanded a fifty-million-dollar donation from the Overseas Chinese Association. In order for our family to contribute to the donation, Yong Cheh helped to sell the jewellery that she had kept safely. Even during those desperate days, she managed to get a good sum of money for it. As I listened to Papa, my heart grew heavier with every word.

Papa added that even though the Overseas Chinese Association failed to raise fifty million dollars, it was a significant amount of money. The Japanese officials were satisfied, and the donation saved the lives of a great number of Chinese men. He concluded that Yong Cheh had not only served our family but the entire Chinese community. Everyone was moved by the story, but I was devastated. I had called Yong Cheh a thief to her face, and it was too late to take it back.

Even though Ma disapproved, Papa engaged a monk to conduct some rituals because Yong Cheh had been Taoist. I was excited when they lit a big bonfire for the rituals. Unfortunately, Ma said I shouldn't be around such things and sent me to bed.

At the funeral the next day, it seemed as if every amah on the island had shown up.

Our family, Siew Cheh, and Eng Cheh walked behind the brightly decorated lorry carrying Yong Cheh's coffin. Behind us, the amahs, clad in their black and white samfu, formed a line as long as I could see. Many people came out of their houses to look as we went by. I thought it was appropriate that Yong Cheh had such a grand funeral procession. She had done a good job her whole life, and she deserved to be sent off with respect.

TWENTY-NINE

The house felt desolate after Yong Cheh's funeral. As much as I could, I took Ming to the garden where we watched Spotty and Brownie root around the grass.

Something was weighing on me, and I was trying to run away from it. After I learned the truth about Ma's jewellery, I realised that what I had told Mr DeSouza about Siew Cheh was not true. As lessons with Mr DeSouza resumed, I waited for a chance to bring it up, but it never seemed like the right time. Or more truthfully, I could not find the courage to do it.

One morning, Ming and I were playing in the back garden when I heard Ma's khakiak clicking on the stone path. To my great surprise, Ma had come to join us. She tickled Ming and chased him around, making him squeal with laughter.

"Be careful of your heart, Ma," I reminded her.

"Don't worry, I'm feeling much stronger," she assured me.

She did look better, her cheeks a pretty pink from running around. As we continued playing, I noticed Ying standing under the frangipani tree. She was watching us again. When Ma wasn't looking, I waved at Ying, wishing that she could play with us.

Ma frequently joined Ming and me in the garden after that.

Papa was thrilled about the change in her. When we were alone, he thanked me for the improvement in Ma.

"But I didn't do anything."

"You've done so much, Bee."

"What do you mean?"

"Dr Oei said that Ma needs a reason to get out of bed," he explained, "and that's what you've given her."

"I have?" I asked, confused.

"Yes," Papa said. "Thank you, Bee."

One afternoon, I was embarrassed to find a stack of Ying's singlets on my bed.

"Who put it there?" I asked Siew Cheh.

"Your Ma. She says that you're becoming a young lady," she said.

"I am not!" I replied crossly, my cheeks feeling hot.

Siew Cheh smiled and winked at me. I loved her so much in that moment that the words tumbled out of my mouth.

"I did something horrible! Can you ever forgive me?"

"Of course!" she replied immediately.

I burst into tears.

"What's wrong, Bee?" Siew Cheh asked, concerned.

I told her everything – how I thought she had stolen the jewellery, how I had told Janet, and worst of all, how I ended up telling Mr DeSouza. Siew Cheh listened quietly until I finished.

"Bee, it was a mistake. I really don't blame you," she said. "But you don't have to feel bad about Mr DeSouza. As an amah, I took a vow of celibacy. I pledged to devote my life to my master and his family. I cannot have boyfriends or get married."

"What kind of stupid vow is that?" I asked, shocked.

"It's part of being an amah, just like our hair bun and samfu."

"And you don't mind?"

"I'm contented with my life," she said with a smile.

"But Mr DeSouza likes you!"

"No, no, that's impossible! Tell Janet she has nothing to worry about," she laughed.

After talking to Siew Cheh, I was finally able to tell Mr DeSouza about my mistake. He was overjoyed.

"Of course, I'm not angry with you!" he said, beaming.

"But I was wrong," I said.

"Of course, you were wrong! We were all wrong!" He laughed heartily. It was great to see his face lit up with a big smile, his eyes sparkling. I did not want to ruin his happiness, so I decided not to mention the amahs' vow of celibacy.

Across the table, Janet scowled at me. I decided not to tell her about the vow either.

THIRTY

I found Ma in my room, looking through my cupboard. She surprised me by saying, "Your clothes are getting too small. Let's see if you can wear Ying's."

I cautiously followed her to Ying's room. She stepped into the room and looked around. To my surprise, she did not break down in tears. She walked straight to Ying's cupboard and opened it. We held our breath as we stared at the rows of colourful dresses. It was like a time capsule from before the Japanese Occupation. Back then, our cupboards were full of beautiful things.

Ma took a deep breath and pulled out a dress that Ying had often worn. It was green with white flowers.

"She was fond of this one. I think it will look nice on you too," Ma said, holding the dress against me. When she passed it to me, tears sprang to my eyes.

"What's the matter?" Ma asked, surprised.

I could only shake my head as I hugged the dress. How could I say that what she did touched the part of me that had always been jealous of Ying, the part that thought Ma could only love Ying?

Ma misunderstood my tears. "Ying has moved on, so we

should too. For a long time, I couldn't, but when you fell ill, I thought I would lose you too ..." Ma bit her lower lip, holding back her tears. "We must be brave," she finally finished.

I nodded and wiped away my tears.

"Now why don't you pick out what you want? If it doesn't fit, we can alter it," Ma said.

She sat on the bed while I looked through Ying's clothes. She had a lot of fancy dresses. I pulled out a gown covered with sparkly sequins.

"Ying wore this for her piano performance last year," I said.

"She complained that it was too flashy," Ma remarked.

"She did?" I asked, surprised. "But all the girls loved it! They couldn't stop talking about this dress."

"She complained about that too. She said that they paid more attention to her dress than her music," Ma laughed. In a more serious voice, she continued, "I shouldn't have made her wear all these fussy clothes. She didn't like people looking at her all the time."

When Ying had stepped onto the stage in this shiny dress, looking so glamorous in the spotlight, I had imagined that she lived in a perfect world. Through our time in school together, the brighter she had shone, the more I had felt eclipsed by her shadow. For the first time, I realised that things had not been perfect for Ying. I put the dress back in the cupboard. Ying was right – it was too flashy.

All of a sudden, Ma hurried to the cupboard and started rummaging around. Finally, she held up a small red box.

"It's still here!" she exclaimed happily.

"What is it?" I asked, curious.

Ma opened the box to reveal a shiny gold brooch. It was a little bee with two red rubies for its eyes.

"Ying picked this out for you. She was saving it for your twelfth birthday. She said it's like your name – Bee," Ma said, smiling.

It was my very own jewellery! With shame, I remembered how jealous I had felt when Ma and Ying had gone to the jewellery shop. Ying knew that I had stolen her hairpin, and yet, she'd still gotten me a present.

"Ma, remember when Ying lost her hairpin?" I asked.

"Of course! She was so upset."

"I'm sorry, Ma. I took it."

"Why, Bee?" Ma asked quietly.

"We had a fight, and you punished me. I felt that you always took her side … always loved her more."

Ma turned away. She went to the bed and started folding the dresses that we had taken out of the cupboard. Had I said too much?

In a low voice, Ma spoke. "Dr Oei warned that my heart would be weakened by childbirth. I was fine after Ying was born, and I enjoyed taking care of her. But after your birth, I became too weak. Siew Cheh took care of you, and she did a good job, so I spent all my time with Ying. Perhaps that made me closer to her. I didn't know that it made you feel this way."

"I felt left out," I told her, tears running down my face.

Ma came over to me. "I'm sorry," she said, "I will look after you from now on."

She put her arms around me, and I hugged her. A shiver ran down my spine. I looked up and saw Ying standing in the doorway. Our eyes met.

"I love you," I said, looking at Ying.

"I love you too," Ma said.

Ying smiled. A beam of sunlight shone on her like the stage

lights which had illuminated her in school. She looked so beautiful. Then, like a mirage on a hot day, she shimmered and faded into the air. That was the last time I saw her.

EPILOGUE

I'm twelve years old today! Already, I feel more grown up.

I bathe quickly and put on the new dress that Ma has made for me. She had to use two of Ying's dresses for the fabric. My favourite part is the round collar because it's the perfect place to pin the little bee brooch that Ying had chosen for me. I comb my hair carefully and clip it with Ying's ruby hairpin. It matches the red ruby eyes of the little bee.

I hear music downstairs, so I know that Mr DeSouza is here with his record player. I'm excited because he promised that he would dance with Siew Cheh at my birthday party. They are engaged to be married.

Not to be boastful, but I played an important part in this. I could see that Mr DeSouza and Siew Cheh were in love, so I persuaded her to give up being an amah. She didn't want to at first, even though Mr DeSouza pleaded with her, but I got Ma and Papa to talk to her. It took some time, but she eventually agreed. Siew Cheh still takes care of our family and lives with us, but she no longer wears the amahs' samfu. Janet still hasn't forgiven me for this, so I'm not sure if she will be here today.

As I go down the stairs, I sing to the Vera Lynn song playing on the record player:

We'll meet again
Don't know where
Don't know when
But I know we'll meet again some sunny day …

I freeze. In the mirror across the room, I see Ying. Straight, shiny hair frames an oval face with a serious expression. A wave of emotions washes over me. I have not seen Ying for more than a year. It seems like such a long time ago when I had spotted her under the frangipani tree, on the day of her funeral. In the early days of the Japanese Occupation, she had comforted me and kept me safe. I am now the same age as Ying was when she passed away. Has she come to wish me a happy birthday?

But suddenly, I realise that I am looking at my own reflection! I laugh at my mistake as I wipe the tears from my eyes. Perhaps I look more like Ying than I thought. I will always miss her, but I remind myself that Ying has gone where she's supposed to be. I know that my own place is here with my family. Papa says that the Allied forces have just won an important battle in Normandy. We are hopeful that the British will return soon, and we will live in Singapore again.

I take a deep breath. In the mirror, the girl who looks so much like Ying smiles back at me. I run down the last flight of stairs, excited to see what's in store for me.

ABOUT THE AUTHOR

Mabel Gan is a writer, director, and producer whose work explores the stories of young people. She is the founder of Big Eyes, Big Minds – Singapore International Children's Film Festival and continues to produce the annual event as well as its sister film festival in St. Louis where she currently resides with her family. She has a Master of Fine Arts in Motion Picture Arts from Florida State University, where her thesis film, *Child Bride,* was a finalist at the Student Academy Awards. She wrote and directed the coming-of age feature film, *Sweet Dreams and Turtle Soup*, and helmed numerous television shows, including *Kids United.*